D1724752

# More Mirrors, Windows, and Sliding Doors

# More Mirrors, Windows, and Sliding Doors

## A Period of Growth in African-American Young Adult Literature (2001–2021)

Edited by
Steven T. Bickmore and Shanetia P. Clark

ROWMAN & LITTLEFIELD
*Lanham • Boulder • New York • London*

Published by Rowman & Littlefield
An imprint of The Rowman & Littlefield Publishing Group, Inc.
4501 Forbes Boulevard, Suite 200, Lanham, Maryland 20706
www.rowman.com

86-90 Paul Street, London EC2A 4NE, United Kingdom

British Library Cataloguing in Publication Information Available

**Library of Congress Cataloging-in-Publication Data**

ISBN 9781475843583 (cloth) | ISBN 9781475843590 (pbk.) | ISBN 9781475843606 (epub)

*This book is dedicated to all of the African American authors included in this volume and in volumes 1 and 2. More importantly, to all of the African American authors whose names we don't know and whose work went unacknowledged or was co-opted by others along the way. In addition, we look to the future knowing full well that there are authors who have emerged in the last ten years who could be included here. Perhaps there is another book down the road that will include them and others who are sitting in their rooms, in coffee shops, or in a classroom planning that next young adult novel.*
*I would like to thank my wife, Dana Bickmore, for her support as I finished this project on the eve of retirement and into the first few weeks of that new life. Also, this book doesn't exist without all of the students over the years asking for recommendations.*
*—Steve Bickmore*

*I want to thank my parents, Reverend Shady and Pearl Clark. They instilled in me a love of reading and the love of Black stories and culture and being unapologetically Black. Thanks for being my constant cheerleaders and celebrating this volume collection. I love you.*
*—Shanetia Clark*

# Contents

# Foreword

*What is your origin story?*
*How do you heal yourself?*
*Describe/Imagine a world where you are loved, safe, and valued.*
　　　　　—Natasha Marin's *Black Imagination* (p.11)

Black imagination is boundless. Even when freedoms are limited and there are no seats left at the table, Black stories and dreams persist in finding the tiniest cracks to flow through. These stories and dreams nourish us and urge us to burst forth and claim our rightful places, to celebrate our continued pursuits, and to imagine our adventurous and radical futures. Black imagination speaks in collective dreams, in the reciprocal sharing and preservation of culture, and the constant pursuit of healing and joyful living.

The Black authors featured in this edited collection represent the growing number of creators who are continuing to push forward to share Black stories with our youth. In the past 21 years, we have seen Black authors published in youth literature double (Cooperative Children's Book Center, 2021) and garner more acclaim through starred reviews and recognition from prestigious youth literature awards. The Black authors writing for young adults, some of whom are included in this book, are not only reaching back for inspiration and connection to the Black authors who have come before, but are also expanding forward into less explored genres of speculation, thriller, humor, and fantastical flights of the imagination. With this expansion, we are treated to even more nuanced and authentic representations of the varied, complex, and vibrant Black experience. It is vital for this expansion of Black voices to be not a trending moment, but a sustained movement.

Educators are important players in the sustaining of this movement, for they are gatekeepers who have an impactful influence over the reading choices of our youth. Educators can participate in the silencing and othering of Black literature by denying their right to be in classrooms and library shelves or highlighting only certain types of stories mainly in the month of February, or they can take part in the process of sharing Black stories by keeping them at the forefront and infusing them throughout the curriculum. This edited volume and its predecessors show the importance of bringing awareness to the variety of Black authors creating for young adults and the ways educators can incorporate these stories into classrooms filled with all types of students.

In this book, you will find Black authors who are writing with purpose and love, helping students grapple with aspects of their adolescent identities and understand the world around them. While the featured authors have written distinctly Black stories rooted in Black culture, these stories are meant for all students to critically engage with, and the suggested story-based activities that accompany each essay are rooted in student inquiry, collaboration, and creativity. You will find numerous activity ideas, including photo journaling, pop-up videos, tableau drama, classroom museums, creative writing, graphic adaptations, and collage self-portraits. The activities included in this volume will empower students to engage in critical discourse about text-based themes and their relevance to history and current society, to make projects using their own critically creative imagination, and to remix narratives to incorporate their own experiences and interpretations.

Steven T. Bickmore and Shanetia P. Clark are educators who are heralding the use of Black young adult literature in the classroom. They have curated the Black legends and pathmakers into volumes one and two and are showcasing in volume three many of the authors who have followed in this legacy and who are making even more room for current and future Black authors. As more educators incorporate the authors and activities included in these volumes, the collective Black dreams of resistance, worth, value, equity, and pursuit of joy will continue to weave into the world, illuminating to all the power of Black imagination and stories.

Jewel Davis
Appalachian State University

## REFERENCES

Cooperative Children's Book Center (2021, April 6). *Books by and/or about Black, Indigenous and People of Color (All Years).* Cooperative Children's Book Center, School of Education, University of Wisconsin-Madison. https://ccbc.education .wisc.edu/literature-resources/ccbc-diversity-statistics/books-by-about-poc-fnn/

Marin, Natasha. (2020). *Black imagination.* McSweeney's, p. 11.

# Introduction

## Shanetia P. Clark and Steven T. Bickmore

As we sit to write this introduction, U.S. Senators are debating or attempting to debate on the future of the John Lewis Voting Rights Act, which will protect the right and expand access to vote. There are Senators on both sides of the aisle who do not think that the right to vote is worthy of protection and do not think that removing obstacles, such as the filibuster, is fundamental to advancing democracy.

At the same time, the COVID-19 pandemic rages on, and the virus has morphed into more transmissible variants. Questions of mask and vaccine mandates and if schools at the PK-12 or university level could and should be open to for children, faculty, and staff fill airwaves and social media. Knowing how the schools are an anchor to society, how can schools and universities navigate the pervasiveness of the pandemic? Fights and protests at local school board meetings for or against masks and vaccine mandates have made the institution of schooling a tinderbox ready to be set ablaze.

With the aforementioned, in 2021, Critical Race Theory (CRT) entered into the national discourse. Some pundits thought that CRT was anti-White. The CRT uproar hit a groundswell when candidates for office ran anti-CRT messages. In fact, Governor Youngkin of Virginia signed an executive order on his first day in office. In part, it said,

> Political indoctrination has no place in our classrooms. The vast majority of learning in our schools involves imparting critical knowledge and skills in math, science, history, reading and other areas that should be non-controversial. Inherently divisive concepts, like Critical Race Theory and its progeny, instruct students to only view life through the lens of race and presumes that some students are consciously or unconsciously racist, sexist, or oppressive, and that other students are victims. This denies our students the opportunity to gain

important facts, core knowledge, formulate their own opinions, and to think for themselves. Our children deserve far better from their education than to be told *what to think.* (Office of the Governor, 2022)

This executive order, in essence, is denying "our students the opportunity to gain important facts, core knowledge, formulate their own opinions, and to think for themselves." Educators, librarians, and authors who want to share facts—even the uncomfortable ones—are being ostracized.

When Nikole Hannah-Jones's *The 1619 Project: A New Origin Story* (2021) was published, a fury ignited because it dared to discuss the vestiges and remnants of slavery in today's society. Putting the historical, political, economic, and social impacts that slavery have on just about all aspects of modern life is important for adults and young people—of all races and classes—to understand. The fight to censor Nikole Hannah-Jones's work, as well as works incorrectly described as being anti-White or anti-heterosexual, gained steam.

In fact, a law that went into effect on September 1, 2021, "as part of an effort by Republican Governor Greg Abbott of Texas to remove from schools any curriculum that critics say presents U.S. history as a narrative of White supremacy. The law specifically forbids teaching the idea that 'an individual, by virtue of the individual's race or sex, is inherently racist, sexist or oppressive, whether consciously or unconsciously'" (Salai, 2021). Districts across the country have attempted—and many succeeded—to pull books they deem are "divisive" off the shelves.

Many of the authors in this collection have had their works targeted and labeled "divisive." They have had their work scrutinized and characterized as dangerous for young people. But what has happened as a result of these unwarranted attacks on the African-American authors who dare to tell stories that center African-American children is that more children, educators, librarians, and parents are working harder to expand access to their stories. There is a great urgency to push back against censors, those who do not think that stories about African-American young people are worthy of being in classrooms and in libraries.

This urgency is why we are so thrilled about the timing of this volume. Similar to the previous volumes, each of the chapters provides an introduction to the author, an analysis of a signature work, and then lesson ideas based on that particular work. More importantly, this collection provides armor against the attacks and resistance toward these books and authors. These chapters are written by classroom teachers, teacher educators, and librarians; therefore, they provide a framework for ways that teachers and caregivers can integrate their works into teaching and learning.

This volume continues our celebration of African-American young adult literature authors. The authors presented here have been popular among students and teachers, librarians, and caregivers since 2000; they are Andrea Davis Pinckney, Coe Booth, Shelia P. Moses, Kwame Alexander, Kekla Magoon, Jason Reynolds, Varian Johnson, Renée Watson, Tiffany Jackson, Nnedi Okorafor, and Lamar Giles. They write across genres, formats, and age groups. One thing we appreciate about these authors is their nimbleness. They write about the mundane of everyday life, first loves, sibling and friend rivalries, and the joys and tribulations of growing up. They (re)imagine the future such as "What would happen if one could stop time?" or coin a literacy framework called "Africanfutrism." These authors are Newbery Medal and honor awards, the Coretta Scott King, the Walter Dean Myers Award, the Schneider Award, The Hugo Award, the World Fantasy and Lodestar Award winners and more.

We hope that you and your students find this volume, as well as the entire series, helpful to your research and your teaching. We foresee that you can use this book and collection to combat those who feel that Black stories, characters, and authors are dangerous. They can provide the language to rebut discriminatory censorship. Finally, we want this collection to (re)introduce you to these authors and their work.

## REFERENCES

Hannah-Jones, N. (2021). *The 1619 project: A new origin story*. New York: Penguin Randomhouse.

Office of the Governor. (2022). *Executive Order: NUMBER ONE (2022): Ending the use of inherently divisive concepts, including critical race theory, and restoring excellence K-12 public education in the Commonwealth*. Retrieved from https://www.governor.virginia.gov/news-releases/2022/january/name-918519-en.html

Salai, S. (2021, October 8). *Texas parents ban children's author in critical race theory clash*. Retrieved from https://www.washingtontimes.com/news/2021/oct/8/jerry-craft-childrens-author-banned-texas-parents-/.

*Chapter 1*

# Andrea Davis Pinkney

*Taking a* **Rhythm Ride** *through Motown*

## Dawan Coombs

*Rhythm is the salt of the Pinkney's life. It pulses through Andrea's words and Brian's art and hums steadily beneath the surface of their everyday routine . . . Whether consciously or not, Andrea and Brian haven't missed a beat.* (Winarski, 1997, p. 40)

Pick up any one of Andrea Davis Pinkney's books and you will realize "rhythm" aptly describes the work of this accomplished writer, editor, and publisher. Whether crafting a novel in verse for middle-grade readers, a picture book for children, or narrative nonfiction for young adults, the pattern and beat of her narration combined with the rhythm of her words results in a melodious combination that ties together her stories and ideas.

But, as the introductory quote suggests, the rhythm Andrea weaves into her stories extends beyond her writing and into the authoring of her life. Described by one interviewer as "a woman who deeply values her family, her friends, and her co-workers, showing appreciation for them in ways that uplift the human spirit," she is noted for her ability to fill multiple roles—mother, publisher, editor, writer, mentor, wife, friend, sister, and daughter—and to fill them all well (Grossman, 2005, p. 404).

Andrea's family encouraged her interests in a variety of areas, but storytelling ran deep in their family traditions. Andrea graduated from high school and enrolled in Syracuse University as a journalism major. After graduating she worked as a writer and editor at several different magazines; at one point she was charged by the editor-in-chief of *Essence* magazine to create an ongoing children's and young adult literature review column.

She realized the dearth of literature representing the lives of African-American children. Andrea asked her then-boyfriend Brian Pinkney (who later became her husband) to illustrate children's books addressing her concern as well as her exasperation at the lack of books available, to which he responded,

> Why don't you write the books! And, Andrea, by the way, what you're doing—coming up with ideas for books—is what those children's book editors do. You should write books, and you should be a children's book editor. (Pinkney, 2014, p. 10)

In response, Andrea began writing.

But she also continued her work as an editor, using these experiences to inform her writing and working it all into the rhythm of her life. As an editor and publisher, she seeks to publish books that "honor the African-American cultural experience" in part because these books were absent from her own childhood (Grossman, 2005, p. 404). In addition to working for publishers such as Hyperion Books for Children, Houghton Mifflin, and Scholastic, Pinkney launched *Jump at the Sun*, the first African-American children's line of books at a major publishing company.

Family also significantly influences the rhythm of Andrea's life. She lives and works with her husband Brian and their two children in Brooklyn, New York. Their relationship and collaboration in their professional pursuits result in a "masterful blending of respect and synergy that carries over into their personal lives" (Grossman, 2005, p. 407). She maintains close relationships with her own parents and siblings as well as her husband's parents.

These relationships and people provide the inspiration for her work. For instance, she describes how the men in her life played a role in the inspiration for one of her nonfiction texts:

> As my brother's older sister, and as the mother of a black son, and as the wife of a black man, I'd become acutely aware of the negative impact this bad press and these stereotypes have—especially on boys who are developing an image of what it means to be a black man coming of age. Even in its subtlest forms, this negativity stitches a corrosive thread into a child's psyche and makes him think he's inferior. Once this belief is established, it's hard to turn it around. (Pinkney, 2013, p. 64)

As a result, Andrea wrote *Hand in Hand: Ten Black Men Who Changed America* (2012).

To date, Andrea Davis Pinkney is the author of over 31 books for young people, including children's picture books, middle-grade novels, and narrative nonfiction texts for young adults. She has received recognition for her outstanding contributions in each of these areas, and the numerous awards her picture books have received include the Jane Addams Children's Book

Award Honor citations, the Carter G. Woodson Award, and the Flora Stieglitz Straus Award for Nonfiction, a Caldecott Honor, as well as recognition on numerous "Best of" lists.

In recognition of the body of her work and contributions to the field, she is a four-time NAACP Image Award Nominee, winner of the George Arents Award from Syracuse University, and winner of the Adam's Prize as well as other recognitions from various universities and organizations. See Sidebar 1 for resources detailing her life and work.

### SIDEBAR 1. AUTHOR STUDY RESOURCES

"Picture This: The Pinkneys Are A Picture Perfect, Author-Illustrator Couple" by Lulu Carcia-Navarro, Samantha Balaban & Beth Novey 8/11/2019. *NPR Weekend Edition Sunday.* https://www.npr.org/2019/08/11/747314346/the-pinkneys-are-a-picture-book-perfect-author-illustrator-couple

"Andrea Davis Pinkney & Brian Pinkney, 'Loretta Little Looks Back'." (with Jason Reynolds). *YouTube.* October 5, 2020. https://www.youtube.com/watch?v=lTwSu7h0_-Y

"NCTE Presents: An Author Talk with Andrea Davis Pinkney." October 7, 2020. https://ncte.org/author-andrea-davis-pinkney/

"Meltdown 2021: New York Times-bestselling due Andrea Davis Pinkney & Brian Pinkney." *YouTube.* March 27, 2021. https://www.youtube.com/watch?v=NRBYFsRolcA

"5 Questions with Children's Book Author Andrea Davis Pinkney." *Understood.* https://www.understood.org/articles/en/5-questions-for-childrens-book-author-andrea-davis-pinkney

"In Conversation: Andrea Davis Pinkney and Brian Pinkney." *Publishers Weekly.* September 10, 2020. https://www.publishersweekly.com/pw/by-topic/childrens/childrens-authors/article/84293-in-conversation-andrea-davis-pinkney-and-brian-pinkney.html

"Meet the Husband-and-Wife Team Behind *Duke Ellington.*" By Traci Swain. *Judy Newman at Scholastic.* http://www.judynewmanatscholastic.com/blog/2020/02/interview-andrea-davis-brian-pinkney/

She has received specific notoriety for her young adult nonfiction, including *Let It Shine: Stories of Black Women Freedom Fighters* (2001), which won

Coretta Scott King Honors; Carter Woodson Book Award—National Council for the Social Studies (NCSS); Society of School Librarians International (SSLI) Book Award and ALA Notable Children's Book. *Hand in Hand: Ten Black Men Who Changed America* (2012) won the Coretta Scott King Award and the Jane Addams Book Honor Award. In her acceptance speech for the Coretta Scott King Award Pinkney explained:

> As I said, I'm a creator of nonfiction. I like facts. So, in addition to believing, I know for a fact that when I put my hand in yours, together we can do what we could never do alone . . . I believe that when joined together, the hands of each and every one of us in this room have the power to change not only America but our entire world. (p. 68)

Pinkney seeks to share the power and change she describes here—the power that comes from sharing facts—with her readers.

## JOIN ME FOR THE *RHYTHM RIDE*

*Rhythm Ride* (2015), one of Pinkney's most significant creations for young adults, embodies the full sensory experience and history of Motown. Listed on the 2015 *School Library Journal* Best Books of the Year list, the 2016 Voice of Youth Advocates (VOYA) Nonfiction Honor list, the 2015 *Booklist* Editors' Choice Books for Youth list, and nominated for the 46th Annual NAACP Image Award Outstanding Literary Work for Teens, this text exemplifies the blending of rhythmic language with historical facts.

Readers not only experience the rhythm in her words, but the text features also allow them to see the places, hear the music, and feel the waves of excitement this music caused as it flooded Detroit and then the world.

The narrator of the *Rhythm Ride* adventure—the Groove—takes readers through the history of Motown in a smooth, rhythmic voice. Modeled after the real voice of one of Pinkney's relatives who worked as a deejay and became a veteran in the music industry, the Groove emphasizes words and ideas through italics, phrases, single-word paragraphs, and a tone that makes readers feel that they are listening to one of the voices of Motown.

The book is filled with short chapters that pack significant details and information into concise 5- to 8-page packages. Each chapter talks about a stretch of the journey through Motown history like a ride on a highway, slowing down to focus on certain elements, and speeding up to emphasize others.

From cover to cover, the layout of the text is very reader-friendly, with chapter titles in the upper corners of each page accented by twisted music staves forming a continuous border along the bottom of the pages, interrupted only by page numbers featured on the label of an album. The black-and-white print and pages complement the sharp, crisp black-and-white photographs throughout the book that feature the singers, songwriters, and performers spotlighted throughout the ride. The text presents not just a history of music, but also of the people, events, and forces that shaped the music and that were shaped by the music.

In addition to compelling and rhythmic narratives, several supplementary features enhance the story and provide a variety of additional resources for readers to explore. A timeline of major events outlines the history of Motown and a selected discography lists over six pages of best-selling songs and albums produced by Berry Gordy, including the year, song, and performers. Additional back matter includes a list of TV and movies produced by Motown Productions that invite readers to see the people and events described in the book.

The sources for each chapter are also included, highlighting additional exploration opportunities for readers interested in the different topics and elements presented in the text. Finally, a list of additional sources—including books, magazines, DVDs, websites, and theatrical productions—offers a comprehensive history of Motown remaining to be discovered. These extensive additional features exemplify how different content areas inform, shape, and respond to one another.

## SOLO, QUARTET OR CHORUS: EXAMINING PEDAGOGICAL POSSIBILITIES IN *RHYTHM RIDE*

The rich language, stories, and history presented in *Rhythm Ride* provide several opportunities for students to participate in additional research and exploration about the people, events, and music presented in this work. Whether working individually, in small groups, or as a whole class, students join in opportunities to craft their own nonfiction pieces that can inform, inspire, and bring about the change Pinkney seeks to create with her own works.

### Solo Work: Individual Research and Writing in the Online Community

*Rhythm Ride* showcases the rich sounds and artistry of Motown's musicians, producers, and writers while presenting the stories behind the hits that made them famous. But if students haven't heard the songs and felt the rhythm of the music, they will likely miss part of the experience. For this reason, it may be helpful to guide students through an understanding of Motown before beginning the research and writing activity discussed later in this section.

For example, beginning the unit with an introduction to Motown and some of the music of the era may help students situate the familiar songs and names within the historical context. Listening to all or part of some of the most famous songs, such as "Ain't No Mountain High Enough" by Marvin Gaye, "You Can't Hurry Love" by The Supremes, "Can't Help Myself" by the Four Tops, or "Ain't to Proud to Beg" by The Temptations, will help students feel the Motown sound. The class could also play "Name That Tune!" Motown style to see how many of the songs and artists are already familiar to them.

Students might also enjoy watching a short documentary that introduces the history. *The Motown Effect* (2011) gives a brief history of Motown, particularly how it contributed to the Civil Rights Movement in the United States. Older students may also enjoy watching Richard Pryor recount the history of Motown as a fairy tale at the Motown 25th Anniversary Show. Both recordings, as well as others resources are available on YouTube and offer a helpful introduction to help students segue into the content of *Rhythm Ride.*

The chapters in the book paint a picture of Motown as a sound, a company, and a movement, but "the Groove" intersperses facts about individual songs and artists that contributed in different ways and times. Using Pinkney's work as a model, students can participate in similar researching and writing activities about their own favorite songs.

Teachers could start by helping students examine sections from *Rhythm Ride* as mentor texts, noting specifically where Pinkney deposits details about artists and songs throughout the narrative. Students should begin by noticing the different kinds of facts and details she includes, but then look at how she includes them and where they are interspersed in the text.

For example, in the chapter "Sunshine on a Cloudy Day," Pinkney highlights Berry's efforts to make the Motown sound available internationally and to grow the pool of artistic talent. Pinkney shares background stories about the Temptations and the Four Tops, as well as how Smokey Robinson crafted the lyrics to "The Way You Do the Things You Do." In each section, students can highlight the facts embedded in the smooth narration.

Next, invite students to select a song from the "Selected Discography" (pp. 139–146) that they would like to research in greater depth. Encourage them to identify information about the song and artist from *Rhythm Ride* as well as through other reputable sources, such as the website "Classic Motown," or articles such as "Motown's Most Successful Music Artists, from Stevie Wonder to The Jackson 5" from *Business Insider.* The sources listed in the "For Further Enjoyment" section of the text (pp. 157–160) also provide a wide variety of websites, magazines, and books that could be used to find additional information.

Throughout the research process, consider teaching mini-lessons on identifying sources, notetaking, restating information in their own words, and plagiarizing. As students read, encourage them to note facts and interesting information about their particular songs and artists. It may also be helpful to teach students to cite the sources of the information they discover and to give them opportunities to write about their findings and then revise their writing for publication.

Finally, provide an opportunity for students to share their findings by submitting them to *Songfacts*, an online searchable database that highlights the stories behind popular artists and songs. Managed and maintained by a team of writers and researchers, fans use the site to research music they love, but students can contribute their findings to the database itself.

Once students register and sign in with their email account, they can "Suggest a Songfact or Artistfact" by entering the song title, artist, and source of their information. Next, in their own words, they enter in the fact they discovered in their own research. The entries are then reviewed and once they have been vetted, they will be posted on *Songfacts* with credit given to the student who submitted it. More information about contributing to *Songfacts* can be found at http://www.songfacts.com/blog/pages/about_us/ #contribute.

### Duet, Trio, or Quartet: Conducting Interviews with Different Voices and Learning from Experts

Students will engage with the history and people featured in *Rhythm Ride* when they get to know the people whose work made Motown famous. This activity invites students to hone their research skills by learning about the background of the musical artists, producers, or other people featured in *Rhythm Ride* by identifying important facts, personality traits, and experiences that shaped their careers. Students will then share their findings in expert groups within the class.

It might be helpful to begin by inviting students to interview their parents, grandparents, family friends, or other significant adults in their lives and ask them what they know about Motown to build connections and foreground their learning in their own experiences. Whether they share their affinity for one of Motown's all-time greatest hits or their memories of a particular artist, students will better understand the influence of this music in the lives of their own family and community.

If students are not sure where to begin, it might be helpful to share lists of "The 100 Greatest Motown Songs" from websites such as Rolling Stone or "The 25 Greatest Motown Songs of All Time, Ranked" from Smooth Radio to acquaint them and those they interview with the music of Motown. Spotify, Apple Music, and other streaming services also feature Motown playlists that highlight the chart-topping music that shaped the United States. Soundbites of many of the most famous Motown songs will likely be recognizable to listeners of all generations.

Based on what they learn as a part of these activities or from their reading thus far, students should select an artist or group they would like to research. Online sources such as *The Motown Museum* or *Classic Motown*, as well as books and articles, offer clear and relevant information about these figures. Students may also draw from the "Timeline" (pp. 133–138) included at the end of *Rhythm Ride* as well as from other sources in the "Source Notes" and "For Further Enjoyment" sections that wrap up the text. Encourage students to also seek out information from some of the online resources mentioned in the individual activity.

Students should compile their notes and synthesize their findings into fact sheets about the lives and careers of the artists they researched. They will then collaborate in small expert groups to teach one another about their findings. Students will need to be prepared to share facts about the lives of those that they researched, including the experiences that shaped their careers, and their feelings and responses to the time in which they lived. It may also be worthwhile to invite students to include a prop that represents an important element of the person's life or work.

On the day of the expert groups, students may participate in a few different ways. For example, students may interview one another, interacting and exchanging information with one another through questioning and responses. Another possible arrangement includes pairing experts on musicians and figures with similar interests and inviting them to speak across time periods and ask questions of one another. Regardless of the pairings, it may be helpful to brainstorm a list of questions beforehand to allow students to prepare and practice their responses.

## Adding to the Chorus: Pop-Up Videos

The research activities described above also provide the foundation for collaborative presentations. Students share their research findings with their classmates using the genre of the "pop-up video," popular in the late 1990s. In this genre, ordinary music videos become exercises in reading as text bubbles pop up throughout the experience, supplementing the music with interesting facts that reveal the stories behind the songs. Beyond their entertainment value, this genre helps fans make connections and extend the meaning of the music they love by blending it with nonfiction. This combination makes it a worthwhile genre for the classroom.

Since most students may not be familiar with this genre, show an example of a pop-up video to model the genre. (Note: Many of these videos are available on YouTube, such as "I'll Be There For You," by The Rembrandts.) Depending on the age and sensitivities of the students, teachers may want to preview videos before using them as models. As they watch, ask students to note the characteristics of the genre, such as the first pop-up that includes the band name, the title of the song, the album, the company that produced it, and the director.

Throughout the rest of the video, encourage them to notice the variety of information the pop-ups contain, including information about the song, the production of the video, facts about the artist, or pop-culture rifts on the content of the song or video. At the conclusion of each video, a longer pop-up fact about the artist or the song appears with the artists' name and title of the song.

Next, drawing on student observations collected during the videos, create a class rubric listing the types of facts a pop-up video contains. You may consider watching more than one video to help students recognize reoccurring characteristics across the genre (other recommended videos include: "99 Red Balloons" by Nena and "I've Got My Mind Set on You" by George Harrison). As a class, decide how many and which types of facts their "videos" should contain.

Then, working in pairs or small groups, assign or let students choose a song featured in *Rhythm Ride* that they would like to use as the focus of their pop-up video. Since most (if not all) recordings of these songs took place before the creation of music videos, students will likely either use a recording of a live performance they find online or compose their own video using PowerPoint that sets the song against a backdrop of images.

Students may include the pop-up element in a variety of ways. If using PowerPoint, text bubbles can be easily added to the slides featuring the researched information. If students don't have access to technology or teaching them how to use these tools would eclipse the focus on research, students may create text bubbles that they literally "pop-up" and hold while a video of the song performance is projected on a screen behind them.

Regardless of what form these final products take, giving students the opportunity to share both the music and the stories of Motown will bring to life the people and the voices of this hinge point in U.S. history and keep them moving toward the final destination of *Rhythm Ride*.

## BIBLIOGRAPHY OF ANDREA DAVIS PINKNEY'S MIDDLE-GRADE WORKS

In addition to the over 20 picture books or novels Pinkney has written and published for young children, she has also penned the following titles for middle grades readers:

*Loretta Little Looks Back.* (2020). Illus. by Brian Pinkney. Little Brown. Historical fiction.

*Martin Rising.* (2019). Scholastic. Nonfiction.

*Rhythm Ride.* (2015). Roaring Brook Press. Narrative nonfiction.

*The Red Pencil.* (2014). Illus. by Shane W. Evans. Little Brown. Novel in verse.

*Peace Warriors.* (2013). Scholastic. Nonfiction.

*Hand in Hand: Ten Black Men Who Changed America.* (2012). Illus. by Brian Pinkney. Disney-Hyperion. Narrative nonfiction.

*Dear America: With the Might of Angels.* (2011). Scholastic. Historical fiction.

*Bird in a Box.* (2011). Little Brown. Historical fiction.

*Meet the Obamas: America's First Family.* (2009). Scholastic. Nonfiction.

"Five Djinn in a Bottle." (2007). In *Be Careful What You Wish For: Ten Stories About Wishes,* ed. by Lois Metzger. Scholastic. Short story.

*Silent Thunder: A Civil War Story.* (2001). Hyperion. Historical fiction.

*Abraham Lincoln: Letters From a Slave Girl.* (2001). Winslow Press. Historical fiction.

"Building Bridges." (1998). In *Stay True: Short Stories for Strong Girls,* ed. by Marilyn Singer Scholastic. Short story.

*Raven in a Dove House.* (1998). Harcourt. Realistic fiction.

*Hold Fast to Dreams.* (1996). Hyperion. Realistic fiction.

## REFERENCES

Grossman, C. (2005). Raising up Andrea Davis Pinkney. *Language Arts, 82*(5): 404–409.

Ortiz, S. (2015). In-conversation with Andrea Davis Pinkney. *Texas Library Journal, 91*(2): 72–73.

Pinkney, A. D. (2013). CSK author award acceptance. *The Horn Book Magazine, 89*(4): 63–69.

Pinkney, A. D. (2014). May Hill Arbuthnot honor lecture. *Children & Libraries: The Journal of the Association for Library Service to Children, 12*(4): 3–14.

Pinkney, A. D. (2018, May 29). *Andrea Davis Pinkney: New York Times Bestselling Author.* Retrieved from https://andreadavispinkney.com/awards/

Winarski, D. (1997). The rhythm of writing and art. *Teaching PreK-8, 28*(2): 38–40.

*Chapter 2*

# Coe Booth

## *Reclaiming Humanity in Stories about Urban Life*

### Desiree Cueto and Wanda Brooks

With a breakthrough novel in 2006 (*Tyrell*), Coe Booth emerged as a talented writer of realistic fiction stories that appeal to a preteen and teen-aged readership. To date, she has written three young adult novels (*Tyrell*, 2006; *Kendra*, 2008; *Bronxwood*, 2011), and one book created for middle-school readers (*Kinda Like Brothers*, 2015). Several of Booth's novels received local and national awards such as the *Los Angeles Book Prize,* the *Rhode Island Children's Book Award,* and the *American Library's Best Books for Children Recognition.*

The young protagonists in each of her stories live in a fictional city very similar to the one where Booth grew up—Bronx, New York. Reflecting on the urban setting and characters profiled in her books, Booth recently posited that children across all backgrounds are advantaged by reading stories about youth who are both like them and unlike them:

> I've had librarians tell me they just don't think the teens they serve would relate to my books, that there aren't any kids like Tyrell or Kendra in their community. That really surprised me. It's as though teens are only supposed to be exposed to books about people with whom they are already familiar. (Shoemaker, 2011, p. 127)

In the remainder of this chapter, a further introduction to Booth's body of work is presented and then followed by a critical discussion of the novel *Kendra* (2008). The theoretical constructs of *home* and *other-mothering* (Collins, 2000) are relied upon to examine the protagonist's sense of self and belonging as depicted throughout the narrative. Instructional guidance for educators who wish to include this highly regarded novel in their English Language Arts (ELA) classrooms closes out the chapter.

## AUTHENTICITY, HONESTY, AND REALISM

Coe Booth writes and prefers realistic fiction. In her novels, she unapologetically chronicles the complicated and sometimes difficult realities of youth living in urban communities with parents of unstable or limited financial means. The settings (e.g., homeless shelters and social-service agencies), plot topics (e.g., absentee parents, teenage pregnancy, and sexual encounters), and, in particular, the vernacular spoken by her narrators remain true and unfiltered. Her stories portray teenagers who talk, think, and behave in ways consistent with some (although not all) youth from similar backgrounds. For this reason, Booth's writing has garnered much acclaim for its authenticity, honesty, and realism.

Likewise, Booth's work has received its share of attack and calls for censure (Chana, 2016). Those who want to ban (or simply choose not to purchase) her novels sometimes question the veracity or appropriateness of the depictions (assuming that teens and preteens are too young to engage with the content of her stories). And, yet, Booth's former background as a clinical social worker (Prince, 2009) led her to personal encounters with youth of the same age who are, indeed, living the kinds of stories she writes. In an interview, she explained:

> I want my work to show readers the complexity of the lives of kids and teens of color . . . My characters are often going through tough, true-to-life situations, and I want readers to see this up close and know what it feels like. It's my belief that it's only through that kind of firsthand knowledge that there can be true understanding. While I never set out to write something that will serve the purpose of changing people's assumptions, I hope my novels give readers a more complete window into the lives—and hearts—of these kids. (Smith, 2015, p. 11)

Admittedly, Booth is writing in a time where publishers are being questioned about their role in advancing disproportionate literary representations of Black and/or urban trauma (Hare, 2013, p. 44). Aligning with Booth's characterization of her stories, however, we contend that her body of writing does not primarily depict the traumas of urban life. Rather, as revealed in the upcoming section, the stories are about negotiating relationships, striving for academic and economic betterment, raising and standing in for families (both biological and not) as well as staking a claim on one's life and humanity.

## LONGING FOR "HOME": *KENDRA*

The theme of home in relation to the maternal is common to African diaspora literature. Coe Booth's (2010) *Kendra* depicts a 14-year-old African-American protagonist whose connection to "home" is intricately linked to the relationships she shares with two mother figures. Kendra lives in the Bronxwood Projects with her grandmother (Nana), and in her own words, "[. . .] can't wait to get outta here" (p. 1). Yet, through her deep disappointment, Booth highlights the estrangement and alienation Kenda feels from her biological mother (Renee) who chooses to pursue higher education over the responsibility of motherhood. In Booth's depiction, home reflects the state of being displaced.

The meaning of home in *Kendra* emerges out of a particular geopolitical context. America's Black communities have long adopted kin support systems as a means of alleviating structural disadvantage and allowing members to strive, despite their circumstances. Communal ways of thinking and being portrayed in *Kendra* helped African Americans survive slavery and beyond. Today, the practice of "other mothering" is evident in the nurturing, and care grandmothers, aunts, and sisters offer one another's children (Collins, 2000). Other mothers provide necessities such as food, shelter, and clothing, and keep children safe until the biological mother can resume care.

Coe Booth recognizes "other mothering" as a common survival practice, but she also complicates it. In an interview, Booth (2008) states, "I wanted to learn more about the kinds of problems grandparents have when they have to raise their grandchildren, so I read about that and talked to women in my neighborhood." In terms of her protagonist, Booth shares, "She missed out on having a mother, and that has left an emptiness inside of her." These concerns are outlined in the novel as Kendra spends most of her days dreaming about and wishing her mother would come back to get her.

From the start, it is evident that Kendra is not content living in her grandmother's apartment. During a conversation with her father's sister, Adonna, who is only a year older than she is, and who attends the same high school, Kendra shares:

> "What am I supposed to do? I still have to stay with her."
> I wanna add, *At least til Renee gets a job offer and decides where we're gonna move,* but I don't want to bring up Renee's name and get Adonna started again. (p. 4)

While, on one hand, Kendra is afraid that Adonna will speak negatively about Renee, it is evident that Adonna's perceptions also serve to validate her own feelings about her mother. Kendra thinks, "Part of me wants to tell her [Adonna] to mind her own business, but I can't. Because the other part has the same questions" (p. 5). She cannot understand why her mother would choose education over her motherly responsibilities.

Throughout, Booth reveals Kendra's strong dependence upon a strained relationship with her grandmother. Nana often restricts Kendra's mobility to their apartment where she can closely monitor everything she does. This social isolation serves as a protective measure against the perceived dangers of urban street life. However, Kendra complains of boredom and also resents her grandmother's harsh demeanor. Beyond that, she is deeply saddened by the fact that neither of her parents are taking care of her. Kendra's father (Kenny) is in her life, but he's not able to raise her or support her financially. Renee, still at Princeton, offers neither the emotional nor the physical security of home.

Essentially, Kendra's parents ensure that she has a shelter with Nana because that is the only place that they can leave her. It is clear from the start of the novel that Kendra has learned to keep her mouth closed around her grandmother in order to peacefully coexist within their home. Inwardly, she bemoans Nana's efforts to regulate her behavior by controlling everything from her clothing to her ability to voice opinions and form friendships. Her inner dialogue reveals,

> Most of the time, when she starts with that, I just tell her I'm sorry and act all good again. Because most of the time, even when she's getting on my nerves, I still feel bad for her, that she's stuck with me. (p. 17)

Instances in which Nana is grilling Kendra about her whereabouts or intentions fill the pages of the novel, juxtaposed with Kendra's secret wishes to be free of her grandmother's disapproval and restrictions. While Kendra may recognize Nana's desire to protect her, she is perplexed about the "danger" Nana perceives and also by the ways in which Nana tries to shelter her. As a result, she spends most of her time avoiding Nana and tries to come to terms with questions and issues on her own. One way she does this is by reading books that contain sexual content.

Even as she reads, Kendra fears the judgment and accusations she will receive if Nana finds her books. Angered by the thought of being pigeon-holed, she says, "Like just because I'm reading these books, any second now I'm gonna start doing what the characters are doing. When she should know by now that I'm not even like that" (p. 12). By professing, "I'm not even like that," she constructs her own narrative about Black, adolescent female identity and resists Nana's judgments.

Early in the novel, we learn that Renee gave birth to Kendra when she was only 14 years old. Nana stepped in almost immediately to relieve Renee of her mothering duties, which allowed her to fulfill her dreams of finishing school. Renee was able to graduate from high school and then college. After that, she decided to pursue graduate studies. When Renee initially made the choice to leave Kendra in Nana's care while she earned a PhD, Kendra believed that reunion was the goal. Yet, it becomes clear that Renee sees education as an opportunity for advancement—to escape the hardships imposed upon her by an unwanted pregnancy.

Other Black women in the community also hope to see Renee succeed. This hope is reflected in the novel in the sacrifices Nana is willing to make to raise Kendra, and also through the responses of neighbors living in their project building. Regarding Renee, an elderly woman says, "A PhD! See, that's the kind of thing they need to put in the papers instead of all that negative stuff they write about kids from the projects" (p. 54). Renee is seen as a superstar for overcoming the odds. Despite her early indiscretion, and the fact that she has left her child behind, the community takes pride in her academic successes.

Both Nana's and Renee's response to Kendra reflects a lifetime of experience dealing with multiple forms of oppression. The concentration of poverty in America's urban Black communities limits opportunities for education and employment. Members who are hoping to "get ahead," like Renee, must often choose to leave home. After leaving, they are not always able or willing to return. We see this as the novel continues and Adonna asks Kendra about Renee, and says, "She got her fancy Ph.D., and there's no more degrees for her to get, right? So what kinda excuse is she gonna have now for not wanting you to live with her?" (p. 4).

Booth underscores Kendra's forlornness through a flashback of Renee's graduation. Here, Renee ignores her daughter and then passes her off as a younger sister. Kendra says, "And I stood there watching her, seeing how happy she was and how everybody wanted to be in a picture with her, and I felt like I was just another person caught up in her glow" (p. 5). Despite her own feelings, Kendra keeps quiet about the true nature of their relationship.

Littleton (2007) writes that slavery created a "forced motherhood experience for black women that defined their existence and influenced their survival" (p. 55). Renee pushes back against societal conditions by getting an education. Reflecting on this, Kendra says, "When I was little, I wanted to be in college because that's where Renee was all of the time" (p. 87). Renee, for her part, found college to be a refuge not only from the responsibilities brought on by teen parenthood, but also from the project life she escaped through education.

After the graduation ceremony, Kendra believes that Renee will finally be ready to take responsibility for her. But, she is not. Renee admits that if she had it all to do again, she would have seriously considered aborting

Kendra. It is not until after Kendra is thrown out of her grandmother's house on suspicion of sexual activity that Renee reluctantly takes her in. Kendra must face some harsh truths that force her to question her place in the world. *Kendra* is unique in that it is a migration story more than a reunion story. When Kendra arrives at her new address on Convent Street to begin a life with a mother she hardly knows and who does not care to know her, she shares,

> She keeps staring at me, and the look on her face is like she's asking me, Who are you? I'm your daughter, I wanna say—but as usual I don't. Not because I'm scared but because I know if I say that she's gonna get madder than she already is. And even though I don't need her anymore, not in that way. I wanna try to make this work because I'm running outta places to go. (p. 193)

Ultimately Kendra is aware that she is unwanted at Renee's apartment. Her life with Renee has always been distant and Kendra has always wanted for something to happen between them—some kind of connection. Being in Renee's tiny apartment only confirms her feelings of abandonment. Upon finding out that Kendra has been sent for good, Renee begins arguing with Nana, who sent her there, "But what am I supposed to do with her here? I don't have enough room. Where is she supposed to sleep?" (p. 195).

The above-mentioned scene becomes pivotal in that it opens the door for Kendra to ask other personal questions of Renee. These include: "If you were fourteen again, and you just found out you were pregnant, would you do the same thing you did before? Would I even be here now?" (p. 218). When Renee answers, "No, you probably wouldn't be here." Kendra is deeply hurt and begins to cry, but she does not stop there (p. 218).

Kendra asks Renee an even more pointed question, "Why don't you want me? I'm talking about now" (p. 219). Renee is not able to answer Kendra's last question. This scene is critical given that home is shaped by particular histories and geographical contexts in which the Black diaspora has suffered marked forms of violence. Kendra's migration to Renee's home reflects her need to confront the forces in her life that threaten her development, her sense of safety, and her feelings of belonging.

The next section outlines ways in which readers might connect more closely with Kendra's (and other characters') needs, wants, and goals throughout the book. It is essential to create spaces that allow students to research the historical and sociopolitical environment that surrounds home for these characters, and also to give readers ample opportunities to process the lived experiences of each character.

## ACTIVITIES

### Individual

*Graphic Adaptations*

Coe's Booth's body of work is perhaps most appreciated for its authenticity and honesty. In her writing, she bluntly exposes real issues in African-American urban family life. At the same time, she invites the reader to "live through" these experiences (Rosenblatt, 1995, p. 228). Characters like Kendra speak as they would to a close friend—in the present tense, using vernacular and even profanity. As a result, readers feel a sense of immediacy and intimacy when they enter the story worlds of these characters. This engagement invites readers to respond by creating graphic adaptations of certain passages or chapters.

Once students have read the book in its entirety, they will select several passages or chapters to reread, focusing on how the protagonist changes, develops, or comes to see her place in the world differently as a result of certain experiences. Using blank graphic (comic) strips or storyboard strips, students illustrate what they imagined while rereading the passage, and include speech bubbles to share the additional insights they gleaned about the character's thoughts or actions. Recasting the text in a different format often allows students to generate new ideas about the character and the storyline. Reflection questions might include:

- How does this adaptation reflect the author's description in the novel? In what ways is it different? Why?
- What more did you learn about the protagonist's journey through this process? What aspects of her life became clearer to you?

Another variation of this engagement is to invite students to create a new character—a friend, a role model, or even a pet—to insert into the storyline. Students follow the same process of using illustrations and speech bubbles to engage the new character in dialogue with the book's protagonist. Reflection questions might include:

- Why did you choose to create a new character?
- What role might he or she play in the protagonist's life?
- How might he/she relate to the protagonist? What support or insight might this character provide?
- How might the addition of this character shape or change the storyline?

## Small Group

### Photo-Journal Character Analysis

Connected to graphic adaptations, Photo-Journals invite students to carefully consider the character's inner thoughts, feelings, or motivations by representing these through a different medium. Engage students by asking them to read and visualize a key scene. Explain to students that they will recreate what they imagine using photography, and are encouraged to experiment with colors, shapes, angles, and so on to represent their interpretation of the scene. Teachers may allow students to use cellphones or provide access to other digital media to complete this activity in small groups. Photographs can then be uploaded and shared as part of a small group or whole-class discussion using these guiding questions:

- What is the mood? What about the color scheme makes you say that?
- What kinds of lines and/or shapes do you notice? What feelings are evoked?
- Describe the composition (pattern/repetition, contrast, balance, movement, emphasis).
- What do you think the photographer is communicating?

A resource for teaching students how to analyze pictures is *Critical Content Analysis of Visual Images in Books for Young People* (Johnson, Mathis, & Short, 2019).

## Whole Class

### Dramatization

Students need to be exposed to diverse literature that is representative of a range of perspectives and helps them to think critically. Rogers (2004) suggested that students should engage in the interrogation of "all the possible configurations between texts, ways of representing, and ways of being, and to look for and discover relationships between texts and ways of being and why certain people take up certain positions vis-à-vis situated uses of language" (p. 7). Dramatization allows students to examine and interpret literature from various points of view and to better understand the human element and emotional responses reflected in the story.

In preparation for this activity, teachers may ask students to conduct additional research into how the character's worldview has developed within a particular sociopolitical or historical context. Students may be asked to act out a pivotal scene from the book such as the moment when Kendra asked her mother, "If you were fourteen again, and you just found out you were pregnant, would you do the same thing you did before? Would I even be here now?" (p. 218).

One student might recite Kendra's lines, while another might act as Renee. The dramatization should reflect a deeper understanding of each character's life circumstances and also how the students might feel if confronted by similar circumstances. While the scene is acted out, members of the class can be prompted to pay close attention to their own emotional reactions. This activity is then followed by a debrief, during which students consider why the characters think and act in different ways.

Possible questions for debriefing include:

- In what different ways did the characters come alive for you as a result of seeing the dramatization?
- How did you identify with the characters during this process? How did the dramatization help you consider life through their eyes? What personal connections did you make? What questions do you still have?
- For those who acted out a character or scene: How did you go about conveying the character's inner thoughts or motivations? How did this support your own understanding of the character? What did you hope observers might notice or understand about the character as a result of your acting?
- What was the most compelling aspect of this activity?

## FINAL THOUGHTS

Culturally protective writing in both African-American children's and adult books grew out of legalized slavery and continued into the twenty-first century. Because Black people have continued to be seen as a collective group rather than as individuals within a group, articulating individual agency has often been difficult (Collins, 2005). In light of this, Coe Booth's work is radical for the way it refuses to be mired by historic notions of respectability and collective group politics.

There were a number of ways Booth could have portrayed African-American urban family life, including sacrificing truth for the sake of racial uplift. Yet, in her own words, she chose to, "show readers the complexity of the lives of kids and teens of color" (Smith, 2015, p. 11). In so doing, her books have raised questions about power and agency and what it means to define self on one's own terms. Educational spaces that provide an environment for constructive discourse surrounding Booth's body of work should be heralded as significant.

## BIBLIOGRAPHY OF WORKS BY COE BOOTH

Booth, C. (2006). *Tyrell.* New York: Push/Scholastic.
Booth, C. (2008). *Kendra.* New York: Push/Scholastic.
Booth, C. (2011). *Bronxwood.* New York: Push/Scholastic.
Booth, C. (2014). *Kinda like brothers.* New York: Push/Scholastic.

## REFERENCES

Booth, C. (2008). Interview: October 2008. https://www.teenreads.com/authors/coe
-booth/news/interview-100908
Chana, J. (2016). YA author Coe Booth on reading to find commonality in the other.
National Coalition against censorship. Retrieved from ncac.org/news/blog/banned
-books-week-ya-author-coe-booth-on-reading-to-find-commonality-in-the-other
Collins, P. (2000). *Black feminist thought knowledge, consciousness, and the politics
of empowerment* (Rev. 10th anniversary edition). New York: Routledge.
Collins, P. (2005). *Black sexual politics: African Americans, gender, and the new
racism.* New York: Routledge.
Hare, Y. (2013). Beyond the friends. *The Horn Book Magazine,* 42–44.
Johnson, H., Mathis, J., & Short, K. G. (Eds.). (2019). *Critical content analysis of
visual images in books for young people.* New York: Routledge.
Littleton, K. (2007). *The world we have won: The remaking of erotic and intimate life.*
London, England: Routledge.
Prince, J. (2009). Keeping it real: An interview with Coe Booth. *Teacher Librarian,
36*(4): 62–63.
Rogers, R. (2004). Critical discourse analysis in education. In R. Rogers (ed.), *An
Introduction to Critical Discourse Analysis in Education* (pp. 1–18) Mahwah, NJ:
Lawrence Erlbaum.
Rosenblatt, L. (1995). *Literature as Exploration* (5th edition). New York: Modern
Language Association of America.
Shoemaker, J. (2011). Nine young adult authors talk about intellectual freedom. *Voya,*
122–129.
Smith, C. (2015). Race Matters: A collaborative conversation. *The Alan Review,*
8–13.

*Chapter 3*

# Sheila P. Moses

## The Legend of Buddy Bush *and Beyond*

### Shimikqua E. Ellis

Like Walter Dean Myers, Virginia Hamilton, and Mildred Taylor, Sheila P. Moses is what scholar Rudine Sims Bishop categorizes as a culturally conscious writer. According to Sims Bishop (1999), "culturally conscious authors reflect the distinctiveness of African American cultural experiences and the universality of the human experience" (p. 7). All of Moses's young adult (YA) novels are narrated by Black characters, in Black communities, with Black speech patterns, and accurately reflect Black cultural values and experiences.

Brooks (2009) notes, "Because literature reflects the struggles, experiences, and aspirations of its creators, it is not surprising that African American children's literature has developed distinct characteristics and has focused to a large extent on affirming African American life, culture, and history" (p. 141). Along with *The Legend of Buddy Bush* (2004), Sheila P. Moses has made outstanding contributions to African-American fiction and nonfiction for adults and children. She is the author of Dick Gregory's biography *Callus on My Soul* (2000), *So They Burned the Black Churches* (1996), and eight novels for adolescents.

Moses's culturally conscious writing style is evident in her popular award-winning YA novel *The Legend of Buddy Bush. The* novel is set in her hometown of Rich Square, North Carolina, and was her first YA novel. *The Legend of Buddy Bush* was a National Book Award for Young People's Literature finalist and named the winner of the 2005 Coretta Scott King Book Award. This novel brought national attention to Moses and her hometown with striking reviews from *Kirkus, School Library Journal, Ebony*, and others.

*School Library Journal* praised Moses's honest portrayal of racism in the segregated south through the voice of her young narrator, Pattie Mae. The reviewer states, "Pattie Mae's coming of age story re-creates the racial segregation and tension of a small Southern community, demonstrates the loyalty of family, and exposes the heartbreak of injustice" (Jones, 2004, p. 150).

Literary critics even compared Moses's novel to Harper Lee's classic *To Kill A Mockingbird* due to the similar themes and racial conflicts in both novels. *Publishers Weekly* review claimed, "With a plot that recalls *To Kill A Mockingbird*, Moses blends the historical Buddy Bush, the stories about him that her grandmother told her plus her own imagination to paint a realistic picture of 1947 North Carolina" (2004, p. 255). The comparison to Harper Lee's bestseller and classroom classic is a fitting honor that reflects the poignant power of Moses's writing. The novel enlightens and entertains parents, educators, and students alike.

The novel's success led Moses to write the sequel, *The Return of Buddy Bush,* in 2006. It never gained the awards and recognition of its predecessor, but did yield positive reviews. *The Washington Post* (2004) described the text as an "equally fine sequel . . . offering a dazzling glimpse of postwar Harlem." The *Voice of Youth Advocates* (*VOYA*) magazine also noted that "the characters are colorful and memorable, with a realistic and heartwarming depiction of the love that can sustain a vast extended family"(2004, p. 11).

Moses continued to write more YA novels—*The Baptism*, *The Sitting Up*, and *Joseph* (2009 NAACP Image Award nominee); each is set in North Carolina. But none of these YA novels rivaled the awards and accolades of her first YA novel *The Legend of Buddy Bush*.

## CRITICAL DISCUSSION OF THE WORK

Set in Moses's hometown of Rich Square, North Carolina, *The Legend of Buddy Bush* is narrated by 12-year-old girl Pattie Mae. Pattie Mae shares the trials the Jones family face when her Uncle Buddy is accused of rape and escapes a Klu Klux Klan lynching. This young narrator illustrates the racism, segregation, and poverty that African Americans faced in rural North Carolina before the Civil Rights Movement.

In her 2011 National Book Festival speech, Sheila P. Moses disclosed that the character Ma Babe Jones was her biological grandmother, and Pattie Mae is a young version of herself, even though the story takes place 12 years before the author was born. When asked about her book, Moses (2011) exclaimed, "It's nothing like a good fiction book of lies!" Moses admits that the real Buddy Bush was not her uncle, but a 24-year-old African-American man that escaped from the Klu Klux Klan in 1947.

Moses revealed that the real Buddy Bush was walking down the street when a young White lady walked past him, and his shoulder touched her shoulder. He was accused of rape and put in jail. Two days later, the Klu Klux Klan broke him out intending to lynch him, but he got away and hid in a swamp nearby (Moses, 2011). *The Legend of Buddy Bush* is a fascinating fusion of fact and fiction.

There is a lack of critical scholarship on Moses and her novels, but her writing heavily emphasizes what scholars consider significant themes in culturally conscious African-American literature. Family relationships and spirituality have been noted as themes in African-American literature. In *Identity, Family, and Folklore in African American Literature*, Lee Wright (1995) explains:

> Slavery and its legacy left an indelible imprint on the nation and on its literature. African American writers were especially attuned to the need to make white readers recognize the humanity of the Black man and the sanctity of the Black family. The Civil War and Emancipation, regrettably, did not bury the old preju-dices and as a result the need for writers to explore and express the Black man's humanity and love of family continued as an important theme. (p. 3)

Throughout *The Legend of Buddy Bush*, Pattie Mae emphasizes the power of family and faith in times of trouble. The novel begins with a letter that Pattie Mae receives from her big sister Bar Jean in New York. Bar Jean and Pattie Mae reveal how Northern relatives stayed connected to Southern roots. In her research on African-American children's literature, Bishop (2012) noted "there is an emphasis on family love, particularly relationships between young children and elders" (p. 11).

It is evident that this young narrator adores her grandparents. Pattie Mae longs to spend time alone with her grandfather and worries about his health. She is excited about helping her grandmother and prefers to be at her grand-parents' house. Furthermore, when trouble comes, this family sticks together. The grandmother warns, "Mer you and Pattie Mae need to stay here until this mess with Buddy is cleared up," so they move in with her grandparents on Jones property (Moses, 2004, p. 102).

Faith has always been a pillar of the African-American community, and Moses displays the significance of faith in times of trouble through the char-acters in this book. Young (1999) remarks that "as a literary tradition African American spirituality fights racism through the narration of three elements: inner resolve, profound insight, and the struggle against oppressive mores" (p. 89).

This theme of faith with "inner resolve" is most evident in Pattie Mae's grandmother, Ma Babe, the matriarch of the Jones family. Ma Babe leans on her faith for strength when she exclaims, "Law got my boy, but they ain't got my soul. We going be all right. That's what the Lord made tomorrows for"

(Moses, 2004, p. 155). Ma Babe's "profound insight" that they will be fine and her prayers encourage other family members.

When Uncle Buddy is wrongfully arrested, readers also see the Black church community rally to support the Jones family. This novel illustrates how the Black church brings the community to disrupt the struggle against oppression. At church, people hold "Free Buddy" signs, and everyone is praying. Church members even show up to sing gospel songs and praise God when the chain gang comes to Jones property. Faith gives these characters hope and encouragement during difficult times. Faith helps these Black characters rise above the constant racism and dire poverty that they face in this story.

Walter Dean Myers (1986) affirms how being a Black writer meant: "Understanding the nuances of value, of religion, of dreams. Capturing the subtle rhythms of language and movement and weaving it all, the sound and the gesture, the sweat and the prayers, into the recognizable fabric of Black life" (p. 50). Moses authentically captures the faith, prayers, trials, and testimonies of the Black characters in her novel.

Furthermore, culturally conscious authors aren't afraid to expose the racial injustice that has permeated the African-American experience in the United States (Harris, 1990). Racism and slavery are traditionally prevalent themes in African-American literature. Scholars Brooks and McNair (2009) argue themes such as the effects of racism, information about the institution of slavery, and struggles for equality are common across African-American children's literature (p. 141).

So, the theme of racism is a necessary evil in *The Legend of Buddy Bush*. The 1947 Southern setting embodies the Jim Crow era of segregation. The main conflicts and settings of the book are saturated with racism. Before the rising action in the story, Pattie Mae asks her Uncle Buddy what the word "prejudice" means. Pattie Mae recalls, "he said when I'm around Ma it means when people of different races don't like each other. When I'm with him it means, 'White folks hate niggers'" (Moses, 2004, p. 74). This definition of prejudice helps prepare readers for the discrimination the characters will face in the book.

For example, on the way to the movies, Pattie Mae describes how segregation is deeply woven into the social framework of her small southern community. This narrator shares what she observes with readers:

> I sit in the car and watch the white folks going in the movie house all dressed up. Of course, they use the front door. It's sad to watch the coloreds in the best clothes they have go in the back door to get their tickets, where Uncle Buddy will have to go, too. (Moses 75)

The devastation of segregation is transparent in Pattie Mae's narration.

In *African American Children's Literature: The First One Hundred Years*, Harris (1990) argues that culturally conscious authors also "represent 'a storied tradition of resistance,' that is while accurately portraying historical facts, they do highlight African American resistance to racism" (p. 551). The grandparents in *The Legend of Buddy Bush* exemplify this storied tradition of resistance. Pattie Mae's grandpa resents the segregation of the movie theater and makes this clear to his granddaughter. Pattie Mae recalls how "grandpa said he was never going to that theater as long as colored folks have to go in the back door" (Moses, 2004, p. 29).

Later, Grandma Babe displays resistance when she refuses to call White people Mister or Misses. When Pattie Mae goes into town with Ma Babe, she mentions that her grandma only refers to the White storeowner by his last name. Pattie Mae explains, "if white folks can't call colored folks by their name with a handle on it, she ain't calling them their first name either, because she don't want them to think she's their friend" (Moses, 2004, p. 89). Both grandparents reveal their disdain for racism and Jim Crow laws.

Another powerful culturally conscious component in *The Legend of Buddy Bush* is Moses's use of African-American Vernacular English (AAVE). Along with recurring themes, the use of AAVE or distinct cultural dialects is popular in culturally conscious narratives (Brooks, 2006). The rural dialect in Moses's book brings these Black characters and their rural southern community to life for readers. Sims-Bishop (1990) remarks that "the most readily recognizable element of African American culture to appear in books is the accurate representation of many structures that identify a speaker as a member of the African American community" (p. 560).

In *The Legend of Buddy Bush*, the narrator explains how all the folks on Rehoboth Road use AAVE. Pattie Mae remarks, "They have their own words, like "dor" for "door," "yes-ciddie" for "yesterday," "yonder" for "over there," and "boot" for "car trunk" (Moses, 2004, p. 43). The dialogue and discourse that Pattie Mae and her relatives use help readers identify their cultural background and the setting. Moses's use of colloquialisms like "yonder," " someteat," and "aint" clearly indicate a rural Southern setting.

In *Reflections on the Development of African American Literature*, Bishops (2012) states that authors also implement cultural stylistic elements such as inventive metaphors, creative imagery, proverbial statements, and naming (p. 11). This text is full of these elements. Moses does this by sprinkling the novel with idioms like "cat got their tongue" and "there is a dead cat on the line." Moses's use of proverbial statements like "I'm going to tear your tail up" and "the church was chockablock full" displays the dynamics of language and the culture of the characters in the novel.

## PEDAGOGICAL FOCUS IN THE CLASSROOM

*The Legend of Buddy Bush* has ample pedagogical potential. Teachers and students alike will find the historical elements, themes, plot, and narrative style in Moses's novel worthy of study. The Lexile score is 760, so the vocabulary in the novel is best suited for sixth- and seventh-grade students. The 1947 setting pairs well with any Great Migration unit. Constant references to social conditions in the North vs. the South, migration, segregation, and Jim Crow laws can provide enrichment for any middle-school history classroom.

Pattie Mae is the same age as the average seventh grader, so this novel gives modern students a glimpse of what life would have been like for an adolescent in the 1940s. Through Pattie Mae, students will be exposed to a time before indoor plumbing, cellphones, computers, and the internet. Unfamiliar terms like sharecropping, outhouses, chain gangs, and moonshine can be discussed and introduced to students for further understanding of the text.

On the other hand, poverty, racism, and injustice are elements which most contemporary students are already familiar. Some students in American classrooms live with struggling parents who rent from landlords. Many students may also live in segregated neighborhoods. Thus, the novel's emphasis on socioeconomic disparities and the benefits of homeownership and land are relatable topics for students.

In *The Legend of Buddy Bush*, the grandparents are extremely proud of the fact that they own Jones property, and they are much better off than the other Black families in town. Pattie Mae explains how "Grandpa is one of the few colored men in Rich Square that owns his own land. Most of the people rent their houses and land from some of the white folks" (Moses, 2004, p. 46). Surrounded by poverty and plantations, the Jones family property symbolizes the power that can be attained through sacrifice and hard work.

This novel also creates opportunities for educators and students to have critical conversations about race. The text stimulates and incites racial dialogues that are long overdue in American classrooms. Like Pattie Mae in the novel, many children question the injustices and irregularities they see in their everyday surroundings and seek answers. Johnson (2006) argues, "If our children feel empowered by participating in discussions of race and racism, perhaps by breaking the silence we can foster social action" (p. 14).

When Pattie Mae questions the meaning of the word "prejudice," it invites readers to reflect on their own interpretations of this term. Moses's novel reveals how segregation, racism, Jim Crow laws, employment discrimination, the Klu Klux Klan, and police brutality terrorized communities. These issues are still relevant to modern students and worthy of discussion. Educators must use culturally conscious novels to celebrate diversity, foster a sense of community, and promote social justice in the classroom.

Moreover, *The Legend of Buddy Bush* is full of the literary elements that English teachers traditionally teach. Narrative writing, plot, and setting can easily be taught through this well-written novel. The descriptive first-person narration is a writing style that often is taught in middle school. Moses's distinguished use of AAVE illustrates how diction and speech patterns help establish character and voice. Moses's narrative is also full of imagery and figurative language that can enhance students writing. Similes like "sleep like a newborn baby" and "black as midnight" encourage students to create their own.

The novel is also a great text to help students explore the essential components of the plot. Readers can easily identify or discuss the exposition, rising action, climax, and resolution of the novel on a plot diagram. Excellent examples of foreshadowing in the text help readers navigate the plot. The elaborate descriptions of settings in the novel can be used to teach students how setting impacts plot and improve their writing. There are not many published units or lessons plans on *The Legend of Buddy Bush*, but some creative instructional activities for the book are provided in the next section.

## TEACHING ACTIVITIES

There are many engaging and beneficial learning activities that teachers can use with *The Legend of Buddy Bush*. Teachers can utilize a wide range of videos, texts, music, and field trips to help students engage with this text and make connections. What follows is a selection of resources and instructional activities for teaching this text.

### Text to Text Connections

1.) Students can read *Getting Away with Murder* or *Mississippi Trial, 1955* by Chris Crowe to compare the plot and settings with Moses's novel.
2.) Students can read *Roll of Thunder Hear My Cry* by Mildred Taylor to compare the Jones family to the Logan family. Students can complete a Venn Diagram for both families.

### Text to Self-Connections

1.) Have students respond to the following writing prompts: How does your family or your personal experiences with law enforcement compare with the Jones family's relationship with law enforcement?
2.) How does your personal definition of family align with Pattie Mae's? In your opinion, does someone have to be a biological relative to be considered family? Why or why not?

## Text to World Connections

1.) Students research the Scottsboro Trial, Emmett Till, Black Codes, Jim Crow Laws, The Great Migration, police brutality in America, or the Civil Rights Movement. Then create PowerPoint presentations on how fictional conflicts correlate with historical realities.
2.) Students select an article that corresponds with a conflict or theme from the novel. Then ask students to write a comparative analysis of the issue in the article and novel.

### *Writing Activities*

1. Identify an injustice or inequity in your school or local community. Write a persuasive letter to the mayor or school principal to protest this injustice and provide solutions. Be sure to cite evidence for ethical, logical, or emotional claims in your argument.
2. Have students create their own urban legend. Share examples of several urban legends with the class. Ask students to define the term "legend" and give examples. Ask students what legends have they heard from relatives or community members. Then allow students to write their own legends and share them.
3. Review the important components of narrative writing and first-person point of view. Have students identify examples of these elements in Moses's novel. Then ask students to consider a time when they witnessed or experienced an injustice or a bully. Have students write a first-person narrative about this experience.

### *Small-Group Activities*

1. Take students to the library and select books on the Great Migration, Civil Rights Movement, and other related topics. Arrange students into groups of three or four. Have students create a historical timeline for the 1940s that includes five significant people, laws/events, inventions, and images. Each group member is responsible for contributing five facts to the timeline. When timelines are complete, have groups share with the entire class.
2. Place students into small groups and assign each group a main character from the novel. Have each group complete a Speech, Thought, Effects on Others, Actions, and Looks (STEAL) chart using direct quotes and examples from the book. After students complete STEAL charts, in groups they will discuss what these character traits reveal about the character they have been assigned. Have each group create a poster for the character and share it with the class.

***Whole Group Instruction***

1. Before reading the text, set the stage with an anticipation guide. Take themes, situations, and concepts from the book and turn them into debatable statements. Read these debatable statements out loud to students. Have students stand on the right if they agree and stand on the left if they disagree with the statements. Instruct students to stand in the middle if they are undecided. After reading each statement, have students verbally defend their position.

2. Take the students to a nearby Civil Rights Museum for a class field trip. There are excellent Civil Rights Museums in Memphis, Birmingham, Atlanta, and Washington, DC. If none are close by, take students on a "virtual" tour of such a museum. Then have students complete a Civil Rights from A-to-Z activity and share. On a notebook paper, students will have each letter of the alphabet going down their paper. Give students 25 minutes to write something they know about the Civil Rights Movement for each letter. To modify this activity, you can provide terms for half of the letters and require the students to complete the rest.

## CONCLUSION

Shelia P. Moses is a pioneer of literature that centers African-American children. This intentional focus, or conscious critical reading, invites young readers to embrace and recognize the fullness of African-American character. Her work draws in the tradition of storytelling, religion, and family. Through Moses's stories, young readers gain new perspectives of the Civil Rights Movement and the Jim Crow era. They learn beyond what the textbooks say. Shelia P. Moses is a pioneer of YA literature, and she and her work must be celebrated.

## SHEILA P. MOSES BOOKS FOR ADOLESCENTS

Moses, S. (2006). *The return of Buddy Bush*. New York: Simon & Schuster Publishing.

Moses, S. (2007). *The baptism*. New York: Simon & Schuster Publishing.

Moses, S. (2007). *Sallie Gal and the Wall-A-Kee man*. Alexandria: Braxton House Publishing.

Moses, S. (2008). *Joseph*. New York: Simon & Schuster Publishing.

Moses, S. (2011). *Joseph's grace*. New York: Simon & Schuster Publishing.

Moses, S. (2014). *The sittin' up*. New York: Penguin Group.

# SOURCES

Bishop, R. S. (1990). Mirrors, windows, and sliding glass doors. *Perspectives: Choosing and Using Books for the Classroom, 6*(3), ix–xi.

Bishop, R. S. (1990). Walk tall in the world: African American literature for today's children. *Journal of Negro Education, 59*, 556–563.

Bishop, R. S. (2012). Reflections on the development of African American children's literature *Journal of Children, 38*(2), 5–13.

Brooks, W. (2006). Reading representations of themselves: Urban youth use culture and African American textual features to develop literary understandings. *Reading Research Quarterly, 41*(3), 372–392

Brooks, W., & McNair, J. C. (2009). "'But This Story of Mine Is Not Unique": A review of research on African American children's literature. *Review of Educational Research, 79*(1), 125–162. doi:10.3102/0034654308324653

Harris, V. (1990). African American children's literature: The first one hundred years. *The Journal of Negro Education, 59*(4), 540–555. doi:10.2307/22953

Johnson, J. (2006). Talking to children about race: The importance of inviting difficult conversations. *Childhood Education, 83*(1), 12–22. doi:10.1080/00094056.2006.10522869

Jones, T. E., Toth, L., Charnizon, M., Grabarek, D., Larkins, J., & Larson, G. (2004). The legend of buddy ush (Book). *School Library Journal, 50*(2), 150. Retrieved from http://search.ebscohost.com.umiss.idm.oclc.org/login.aspx?direct=true&db=aph&AN=12207155&site=ehost-live&scope=site

*Kirkus*. (2003). The legend of Buddy Bush [Review of the book by Sheila P. Moses], Kirkus, p. 1361. Retrieved from https://www.kirkusreviews.com/book-reviews/sheila-p-moses/legend-of-buddy-bush/.

Library of Congress. (2011). *Sheila P. Moses: 2011 National Book Festival.* [video file]. Retrieved from https://www.youtube.com/watch?v=YQu53RRSX-U

McCray, C., Grant, C., & Beachum, F. (2010). Pedagogy of self-development: The role the black church can have on African American students. *The Journal of Negro Education, 79*(3), 233–248. Retrieved from http://www.jstor.org.umiss.idm.oclc.org/stable/20798346

McLeod, C. A. (2008). Class discussions: Locating social class in novels for children and young adults. *Journal of Language and Literacy Education* [Online], *4*(2), 73–79.

Moses, S. (2004). *The Legend of Buddy Bush.* New York: Simon& Schuster Publishing.

Myers, W. D. (1986, November 9). "I actually thought we would revolutionize the industry." sec.7, p. 50.

Smith, K. (1994). *African American Voices in Young Adult Literature: Tradition, Transition, Transformation.* London: Scarecrow Press Inc.

Smith, K. (2002). Introduction: The landscape of ethnic American children's literature. *MELUS, 27*(2), 3–8. Retrieved from http://www.jstor.org.umiss.idm.oclc.org/stable/3250598

Wright, L. (1995). *Identity, Family, and Folklore in African American Literature.* New York: Garland Publishing.

Young, J. U., III. (1999). Dogged strength within the veil: African-American spirituality as a literary tradition. *The Journal of Religious Thought, 55*(2–1), 87–107. Retrieved from http://search.ebscohost.com.umiss.idm.oclc.org/login.aspx?Direct =true&db=rfh&AN=ATLA0001429928&site=ehost-live&scope=site

## Chapter 4

# "As In" An Award-Winning Writer

## *Kwame Alexander*

### Bryan Ripley Crandall

Recently, a set of Kwame Alexander's Newbery Award-winning novel, *The Crossover*, arrived at a middle school in Bridgeport, Connecticut. The teachers were in collaboration with a National Writing Project site to enhance literacy instruction and, as part of the partnership, eighth grade students participated in writing workshops, including the poetry of Kwame Alexander. During one of the exercises, an eighth grade ELA teacher noticed something remarkable. "They're writing," she observed. "Every one of my students is writing. And they're engaged."

At the same time, an eighth grade male with braids, and the early signs of an adolescent goatee, picked up Kwame Alexander's *Booked* (the only copy in the room) and asked his teacher if he could take it home to read. She was flabbergasted. "He's a nonreader," she reflected. "I need more of these books in my room."

The teacher's reaction parallels many who have introduced the writing of Kwame Alexander to young people. His words are gifted with charisma and intrigue readers of all ages. He composes books that appeal to the humanity in us all (see table 4.1).

A Kwame Alexander text easily fits into curriculum, especially in the units of storytelling, Bildungsroman, poetry, and language. His poetic narratives provide a pulse to the adolescent experience and, with wit and lyricism, appeal to a new generation of readers. He writes the books students *want* to read. In his own words (2016),

> If we don't give children books that are literary mirrors as well as windows to
> the whole world of possibility, if these books don't give them the opportunity to
> see outside themselves, then how can we expect them to grow into adults who
> connect in meaningful ways to a global community, to people who might look
> or live differently than they. You cannot.

**Table 4.1   Kwame Alexander's Published Work**

---

**Books for Teens**

Alexander, K. & Patterson, J. (2020). *Becoming Muhammad Ali*. New York: Jimmy Patterson Books & HMH

Alexander, K. (2020). *Light for the World to See: A Thousand Words on Race and Hope*. New York: HMH

Alexander, K. & Anayabwile, D. (2019). *The Crossover*. New York: HMH Books for Young Readers (graphic novel)

Alexander, K. (2018). *Rebound*. New York: HMH Books for Young Readers

Alexander, K. & Hess, M.R. (2018). *Swing!* New York: Blink Books

Alexander, K. & Hess, M.R. (2017). *Solo*. New York: Blink Books

Alexander, K. (2017). *The Playbook: 52 Rules to Aim, Shoot, and Score in This Game Called Life*, photographed by Mr. Thai Neave. New York: HMH Books for Young Readers

Alexander, K. (2017). Seventy-six dollars and forty-nine cents. In E. Oh's (ed.) *Flying Lessons and Other Stories*. New York: Penguin Random House

Alexander, K. (2016). *Booked*. New York: HMH Books for Young Readers

Alexander, K. (2014). *The Crossover*. New York: HMH Books for Young Readers

Alexander, K. (2013). *She Said, He Said*. New York: Amistad Press

**Books for Children**

Alexander, K. (2020). *Kwame Alexander's Free Write: A Poetry Notebook*. Illinois: Sesame Street Workshop

Alexander, K. (2019). *How to Read a Book,* illustrated by Melissa Sweet. New York: HarperCollins Press

Alexander, K. (2019). *The Undefeated,* illustrated by Kadir Nelson. New York: Versify

Alexander, K. (2017). *Out of Wonder: Poems Celebrating Poets* (2017), illustrated by Ekua Holmes, with Chris Colderley and Marjory Wentworth. Massachusetts: Candlewood Press

Alexander, K., Hess, M.R. & Nikaido, D. (2017). *Animal Ark,* photographed by Joel Sartore. Washington, DC: National Geographic Kids

Alexander, K. (2016). *Surf's Up,* illustrated by Daniel Miyares. New York: NorthSouthBooks

Alexander, K. (2011). *Acoustic Rooster and His Barnyard Band,* illustrated by Tim Bowers. Michigan: Sleeping Bear Press

Alexander, K. (2010). *Indigo Blume and the Garden City,* illustrated by JahSun. California: CreateSpace Independent Publishing

**Resources for Writing Teachers**

Alexander, K. (2018). *The Write Thing: Kwame Alexander Engages Students in a Writing Workshop (and You Can Too!)*. Texas: Shell Education

Weissman, E.B. & Alexander, K. (2017). *Our Story Begins. Your Favorite Authors and Illustrators Share Fun, Inspiring, and Occasional Ridiculous Things They Wrote and Drew As Kids*. New York: Atheneum Books

Alexander, K. (2016). *Kwame Alexander's Page-to-Stage Writing Workshop*. New York: Scholastic

Alexander, K. & Foxx, N. (2002). *Do the Write Thing: 7 Steps to Publishing Success*. Washington, DC: Manisy Willows Books

His writing provides a doorway for many to enter a reading world. Alexander's originality soars on every page.

A single copy of *The Crossover* or *Booked* distributed within a classroom begins a reading frenzy. Kids share the books, recommend them, and make requests to read similar ones. As New Haven, Connecticut, teacher Donna Delbasso remarked, "It has never been a *normal* or acceptable practice for kids at our school to be scrambling for books in the library. I'm just going to put that out there. Fighting over books is not a typical behavior of our students" (Crandall et al., 2016). Yet, that is exactly what happened (and does happen) when Alexander's books arrive.

## AWARD-WINNING WORDS

Alexander's writing represents the best in young adult literature and, upon success of *He Said, She Said* (2014), he turned to poetic narratives that offer tremendous utility for instruction. His writing has been the missing link needed in the middle and high school curriculum, as it appeals to athletes, word-lovers, romantics, and angst-filled youth, alike. He offers rhythmic narrative arcs with the pitter-patter of language. *The Crossover* (2014), *Booked* (2016), *Solo* (2017), *Rebound* (2018), and *Becoming Muhammad Ali* (2020) offer a way for teachers to make poetry credible, approachable, and pedagogically useful for students.

Kwame Alexander's *The Crossover* is about a young Black teenager, Josh Bell, who is on the cusp of adolescence and finds himself "crossing over" into adulthood. A choice Josh makes at a basketball game runs perpendicular with his family's values and results in a conflict that he must face. A relationship with a twin brother, the passion for his sport, and his respect and admiration for his parents—annoying and tough as they are—provides an appealing storyline for adolescent readers: one that Cornelius Eady (2014) acknowledged is "most boldly and certainly a book about tenderness."

In *The Crossover*, Josh is the "MYTHical MANchild" (p. 10) who is reminded, *"There are always consequences"* (p. 140). The tenderness results, however, from the relationship between his father's "hypertension" (p. 76) and his "dazzling crossover" (p. 226)—his well-respected basketball maneuver. In the end, he realizes, "True champions/learn/to dance/through/the storm" (p. 230).

Kwame Alexander, the poetic and master storyteller, is the "Yes" man who seizes the day (Giovanni, 2015). As a poet, novelist, educator, and human being, he is a visionary whose commitment spreads literacy around the world through (1) *Leap for Ghana*, an initiative with cofounder Tracey Chiles McGhee; (2) *Book in A Day*, a literacy program that celebrates and encourages creativity in youth; (3) *Kwame Alexander's From Page To Stage Writing Workshop* (2016); and (4) his advocacy that poetry is "an answer" for planting seeds of both "diversity and equity" and "empathy and unity" (*New York Times*, 2016).

*The Crossover* received the 2014 John Newbery Medal and Coretta Scott King Author Award Honor for enhancing diversity, equity, empathy, and unity. The writing is celebrated because it engages a new generation of readers, assists any educator interested in an equity framework for culturally and historically responsive literacy (Muhammad, 2020), and offers a "new ballgame" for sports enthusiasts and cultural critics (Brown & Crowe, 2014). It is a text to promote community dialogue and democracy (Crandall, 2016c) and to help turn K-12 literacy programs around (Crandall, 2016b).

## AT THE FREE-THROW LINE, IN A HUDDLE, AND CUTTING THE NET TOGETHER

Kwame Alexander's *The Crossover* presents pedagogical possibilities to assist adolescent readers and writers. The following individual, small group, and whole-class activities are ways young people might cross over with critical thinking and creativity on their own. Kwame Alexander's styles of poetry provide multiple models for young people to explore and try.

### Individual Activity: *As In, A Free-Throw Line*

It is relevant to use Kwame Alexander's *The Crossover* to encourage students to write poetry—a solo performance. The following activity requires a teacher to give students an opportunity to "go to the free throw line" and take a shot at their own poetic basket. The lesson requires 45–60 minutes. Teachers should pre-select poems from *The Crossover* that will prompt discussions about Alexander's style and techniques. The lesson here is specific to "As In" poems found in *The Crossover* (pp. 29, 39, 48, 55, 76, 104, 118, 142, 154). Students should read these poems, analyze them for style, then write one on their own.

Here, teachers should use the "As In" poems to model what Kleon (2012) argues to do in *Steal Like An Artist* and what Gallagher (2006, 2015, 2011) encourages teachers to do when teaching adolescent writers. That is, students should analyze and think critically about an author's craft, and try to replicate similar styles in their own writing. The purpose for this lesson, then, is to have students craft an original poem that follows one of Kwame Alexander's styles.

## MODEL 1: AN "AS IN" POEM

**free-throw line**
[free-layhn throh] *noun.*

The location on a basketball court
where a player is given an unopposed attempt
to score in exchange for an opponent's foul.

As in: The player, a solo act,
dribbles twice from the *free-throw line*,
keeping eyes on the rim,
before shooting to tie the championship game.

As in: Part of what teachers do as coaches
is to encourage youth to take linguistic shots
from *a free-throw line*, to go solo,
in the game of literacy.

As in: Have students discuss
poetic devices before
they bounce language at their own *free-throw line*
and compose a poem on their own.

For example, a teacher could read "Cross-o-ver" (p. 29) with students and ask them to notice how the poem works. What choices did Kwame Alexander make as a writer, and what might they note about his word choice and layout? Students will likely note that a single word is used as a title, followed by a phonetic spelling, whether it is an adjective, verb, or noun. They can see that the stanza that follows is a definition of the word, where Alexander drops lines for rhythm and layout. They will see, too, that a repeat of the words "As in" follows and offers three more stanzas, where the word is further defined with real-world and personal explanations.

## MODEL 2: STUDENT "AS IN" POEM

**Hangry**
Han-Gry [hayn-GREE] *adjective.*

An emotion that occurs
when an emotional person
needs food **PDQ** [pretty darn quick] and
lashes out unintentionally at
others around them.

As in: When done at the
wrong moment and
to the wrong person,
*hangry* can ruin everyone's day, PDQ,
and start a chain reaction.

As in: Paula Dean,
Paris Hilton
and Naomi Campbell
probably just *hangry*
cuz they need a Cinnabon, PDQ.

As in: I was super *hangry*
when I yelled at my dog
GET OUT NOW!
and he ran away, PDQ
(once the *hangry* person is given food
they better apologize, PDQ, too)

Teachers should prompt students on what they notice: (1) *What patterns are seen?* (2) *What punctuation does Alexander use?* (3) *Where does Alexander break lines?* (4) *What can be stolen from his writing?* They should instruct students to read two or three of the "As In" poems for analysis. A teacher might model their own "As In" poem, too, as I've done with "free-throw line" (see Model 1—Teacher "As In" Poem). Such an exercise develops vocabulary at the same time it showcases craft. Students might even define slang words popular to youth communities, as one seventh grader did with the word "Hangry" (see Model 2—Student "As In" Poem).

The "As In" poems are one of many patterned in *The Crossover* to tell the story of Josh Bell. Teachers might choose to explore other Kwame Alexander styles (e.g., "Dialogue" poems and "Rule" poems, also discussed in this chapter). The goal for these exercises, though, is to have students read several poems for inspiration to write their own. Let them be poets, too.

## *Small-Group Activity: As In, the Huddle*

The following small group activity encourages dialogue and helps establish democratic practices. The lesson asks students to "huddle" for approximately forty-five to sixty minutes. A teacher plays a timekeeper and notetaker. Central to the lesson, however, is a teacher-designed dialogue booklet (Probst, 2007; Crandall, 2016a). This booklet contains a series of questions written to prompt students to talk with one another about a book. The goal is to offer an opportunity for a group of three to five individuals to participate in a conversation that helps a classroom teacher reach a larger goal in the unit (see table 4.2).

### *A DIALOGUE-BOOKLET*

*Be strategic:*

1. Think of eight to ten open-ended questions.
2. Have an overall objective in mind.
3. Word-process questions in two columns.
4. Mix questions: text to text, text to self, and text to world.
5. Create questions to prompt dialogue.
6. Write the last question to lead the small groups to report to the whole class.
7. Cut questions into small pages to make a small booklet
8. Staple the pages.
9. Distribute.
10. Listen to their conversations.

**Table 4.2   Sample Questions for a Dialogue Book**

| | |
|---|---|
| Introduce yourself to the group. Offer a statement about yourself and your world. Share any nicknames you have (like Josh Bell's *Filthy McNasty*). | Someone in the group, model what a "crossover" looks like in a basketball game. In what ways do characters "cross over" within Alexander's text? How does a "crossover" work as a metaphor? Are sports, in general, a metaphor for life? Why or why not? |
| Time to do some rating (10 is high, 1 is low). On a scale of 1–10, what is your relationship to poetry? To vocabulary? On a scale of 1–10,  how do you rate *The Crossover*? Why? | Reread "Free Throws" (pp. 234–237). What is a free throw? When do players make them in a game? Why do you think Kwame Alexander ends the book with this poem? In what ways does it bring closure to Josh and Jordan Bell? |

Teachers might create ten questions specific to *The Crossover* or blend questions relevant to themes of the book with the youth cultures they serve (see A Dialogue Booklet). According to Probst (2007), the questions should not be dead-ended or yes/no, and "designed to move a group through a conversation, allowing the students a great deal of control over what they discuss but not abandoning them entirely" (p. 55). Rather, teachers craft open-ended questions to elicit ideas and prompt group members to think aloud in response to one another. Classroom talk is prompted intentionally.

A teacher might choose to model a "dialogue poem" from *The Crossover* as one way to introduce the dialogue booklets. For example, "Walking Home" (p. 58) is a poem written in two voices. It is a conversation between JB and Jordan that should sound familiar to the banter of youth. Kwame Alexander uses this poetic style throughout the book (pp. 6, 16, 17, 58, 74, 96, etc.). Teachers could highlight the conversational nature of these poems to introduce how Alexander uses dialogue between individuals to move a narrative along.

In "Walking Home," JB and Josh converse as brothers often do. They ask questions, offer curt replies, and meander through friendship, frustration, sarcasm, and wit. In the poem, Josh is questioning JB about the championship game, yet also probing for information about their father's health issues. Alexander uses a regular font for when Josh speaks and font in italics when JB speaks. It offers realistic language and voice, yet also provides more to the story.

## MODEL 3: TEACHER DIALOGUE POEM

**Dialogue With My Self**
Hey, Bryan. Who are you talking to?
*Readers in my head.*
Readers in your head? How'd they get there?
*Imagination. Experiences as a teacher and researcher.*
An imagined audience, huh?
*Yes, Because I'm writing about The Crossover.*
Kwame's book again?
*Yep. Conversational stuff. The Dialogue books.*
They'll want to know how to make them.
*I know. I know. I'm getting there.*

Similar to Kwame Alexander's "As In" poems, a teacher should introduce the dialogue activity by reading a few two-voice poems. They should ask,

"What is Kwame Alexander doing here?" The students will likely respond that Josh and JB are having a conversation, which is the great segue toward the objective of the dialogue books, where students will participate in small-group conversations. While students talk, the teacher should wander and join conversations where appropriate. On a notepad, they might jot down the notes of what they hear. It is okay if students don't complete all the questions and stray from the booklet. The goal is to talk.

Dialogue booklets encourage interpersonal, listening, and reflective skills, all while emphasizing the importance of dialogic practices (Fecho & Botzakis, 2007). Further, teachers should draw attention to how Alexander uses dialogue in *The Crossover* as another poetic style. A teacher might craft a two-voice poem of their own model (see Teacher Dialogue Poem). They might even assign students to write one for homework—a poem with two voices in mind on a topic that is pertinent to the student writer.

## Whole-Class Activity: As In, Cutting the Net Together

This final activity is intended for the whole class to culminate new learning at the end of a unit. Here, students make a connection between what they learned from Alexander's book with a larger written outcome or presentation. Choice is extremely important. Students are told that the final project is assigned to showcase original thinking from every member in the class and will be shared with others. The end-of-a-unit expectation requires one to three 45–60 minute blocks, depending on how the teacher assigns the culminating work.

A third poetic style used in Kwame Alexander's *The Crossover* are the "Rules" poems (pp. 20, 51, 66, 71, 93, 129, 146, 191, 214, and 230). These are basketball rules he later expanded into his publication, *The Playbook: 52 Rules to Aim, Shoot, and Score in This Game Called Life (2017)*. In *The Crossover,* however, Josh applies ten basketball rules to his own life, another style of writing that can be analyzed with students.

For example, Kwame Alexander writes "Basketball Rule #7," where he narrates a connection between being self-aware and making a rebound from the backboard. It is a life lesson that an athlete should never forget. The rules of basketball help Josh Bell to create a personal philosophy for living his own life. For example, in this poem, Josh learns "you can't drop the ball" (p. 146). Students should be instructed to read all the "Rules" poems collectively. Parallel to the analysis of the "As In" and the "Dialogue" poems, students should discuss what they notice. They should determine that the poems offer a list for being successful in basketball, as well as life.

## MODEL 4: TEACHER LIST POEM

**List Rule #1**
Making a list
requires thinking,
scratching the head
and jotting down
laws for what's
to be done
to make an idea, action,
or passion
possible.
Rules matter.
They are a pathway
for feeling accomplished,
especially when crossing
them out.

Teachers, again, might model their own "list poem" (see Teacher List Poem). Rules abound everywhere and can be tapped for writing purposes. Such rules are often what young people complain about most. Yet, Alexander uses rules so that Josh Bell makes a larger connection for a better life. That's the originality of such poems.

As an introduction to the culminating project, a teacher should have students trace their hands onto a piece of paper. They should then ask students to number each finger. One way to prove the importance of rules is to have students name any topic that interests them and to list ten rules that exist for it, one for each finger. The students should be told that at the end of reading *The Crossover*, they are to create their own series of "Rules" poems on a topic of their choice.

The culminating project prompted by *The Crossover* is for everyone to focus on one set of rules that exists for something they are passionate about. First, they must think through rules for their chosen topic (e.g., Rules for Listening to Hip Hop, Rules for Dance Class, Rules for a Soccer Field). The second part is to have students work with these rules and, like Kwame Alexander, explore them poetically. The third and final part is to have students think creatively on how to present their work (e.g., PowerPoint, StoryMap, Padlet, Comic Book, Spoken Word).

For older readers, an alternative option is to develop an essay where the author narrates more about their chosen topic, with discussion of the rules associated with it. Here, students might develop personal stories to justify the rules and how they learned them. Such essays can be personal, or with older students, allowing for research with expertise from knowledgeable sources (e.g., a student choosing to write rules for getting into college might access websites, interview adults, and cite articles as justification for why such rules matter).

The teacher should explain, however, that the culminating project will be to teach others in the class about the topic they chose to write about. Teachers should emphasize the importance of making lists as a brainstorming practice. Teachers might also encourage students to draw their rules as a means for visual, illustrative communication (Fisher & Frey, 2016). Students might even share their rules as Tweets or memes. Having options enhances how students wish to express themselves.

On the day of presentations, too, a teacher might show a clip of an NCAA champion team cutting down a net after winning a national title. Students should be reminded that it is not a single player that removes the net, but the entire team and the coaching staff at their side. It's everyone working together on a goal, just like the culminating projects for *The Crossover* unit. Interacting with Kwame Alexander's writing is a team effort, where every individual contributes to the larger community.

## As In, Crossing Over with a Final Thought

Adolescence is traditionally viewed as a period between childhood and adulthood where young people "cross over" into more intellectual thinking, curiosity, and responsibility. Reading *The Crossover* with students, then, is a way to think, laugh, speak, share experience, worry, and wonder with young people as they explore poetic language and a love of words for themselves.

Kwame Alexander, with his rhythmic and poetic brilliance, provides readers with exemplary writing that should be celebrated. His writing demonstrates how verse, like music, tells a story and provides a location for teachers to stop and think about the importance of word choice with students. He writes books to make poetry come alive in our rooms.

*The Crossover* rapidly defied all the critics who told Kwame Alexander that adolescent males would never read poetry and adolescent females would not enjoy a book about basketball. Lucky for all, young people proved these naysayers wrong. As a result, Kwame Alexander helps school-aged youth cross over into a lifetime of reading. His body of work has filled tremendous gaps—it is creative storytelling that has been needed for a very long time.

# REFERENCES

Alexander, K. (2016). Kwame Alexander on children's books and the color of characters. *New York Times: Author's Note.* April 26.

Brown, A., & Crowe, C. (2014). From the guest editors: A whole new ballgame: Sports and culture in the English room. *English Journal, 104*(1): 11–12.

Crandall, B. R. (2016a). Promoting democracy through sports, community, and dialogue with Kwame Alexander's the crossover. In *Developing Contemporary Literacies through Sports: A Guide for the English Classroom*, edited by A. Brown and L. Rodesiler. Urbana, IL: National Council of Teachers of English.

Crandall, B. R. (2016b). "'Taking risks' with digital acoustics." *Study and Scrutiny, 1*(2): 100–125.

Eady, C. (2014). Heart of a champion: "The Crossover" by Kwame Alexander. *Sunday Book Review: New York Times.* May 9th, retrieved online at https://www.nytimes.com/2014/05/11/books/review/ the-crossover-by-kwame-alexander.html?_r=0

Fecho, B., & Botzakis, S. (2007). "Feasts of becoming: Imagining a literacy classroom based on dialogic beliefs." *Journal of Adolescent & Adult Literacy, 50*(7): 548–558.

Fisher, D., Frey, N., & Hattie, J. (2016). *Visible Learning for Literacy, Grakes K-12: Implementing the Practices That Work Best to Accelerate Student Learning.* Thousand Oaks, CA: Corwin Press.

Giovanni, N. (2015). Kwame Alexander. *The Horn Book Magazine, 91*(4): 78–79.

Muhammad, G. (2020). *Cultivating Genius: An Equity Framework for Culturally and Historical Responsive Literacy.* New York: Scholastic.

Probst, R. E. (2007). Tom Sawyer, teaching and talking. In *Adolescent Literacy; Turning Promise into Practice*, edited by K. Beers, R. E. Probst and L. Rief. Portsmouth, NH: Heinemann, pp. 43–49.

*Chapter 5*

# From Ordinary to Extraordinary

## *Kekla Magoon*

### Kimberly N. Parker

Kekla Magoon's writing champions the "un-hero." With an audience of readers ranging from middle grade to young adult, and genres spanning historical fiction, fantasy, contemporary realistic fiction, short stories, and nonfiction, Magoon's work consistently and intentionally presents stories of complex, everyday characters. In her effort to correct misunderstandings about Black history for her young readers, Magoon encourages young people to see themselves as able to create change in their own worlds.

This chapter examines Magoon's elevation of the ordinary, everyday characters in her acclaimed works of historical fiction, biography, and contemporary realistic fiction. Magoon's insistence on expanding the possibilities of African-American children's literature is a political decision, and her activism has pushed the publishing industry to respond to the needs of diverse audiences. This chapter concludes with activities educators can use to encourage young people to consider how Magoon's literature can support powerful explorations of self, history, and change. Her insistence on creating narratives and voices that are often overlooked is a powerful counternarrative that Black readers, and many others, deserve.

### WRITING THROUGH HER QUESTIONS: THEMES

Magoon has consistently portrayed characters that are complex, situations that are nuanced, and historical moments that encourage revisiting and rethinking. She has earned high praise for centering the voices of protagonists of color, especially African-American ones, in her work. She has received the Margaret A. Edwards Award, the Boston Globe-Horn Book Award, the John Steptoe New Talent Award, three Coretta Scott King Honors, the Walter

Award Honor, an NAACP Image Award, and has been a finalist for and long-listed for the National Book Award.

Magoon's writing often comes from her own desire for a more robust historical knowledge beyond what she learned in school. In her essay "Why I Write" for the National Writing Project (2014), she explains her motivation for writing *The Rock and the River*: "I wanted to imagine what it felt like to exist at that moment in time and to have to make a choice about where you would stand, and what you would stand for." Magoon's inquisitiveness fueled a novel that answers the questions many readers have about why history matters and its importance to the modern day. Additionally, it is this book that received Magoon's first round of critical attention and awards.

Magoon's research for *Rock* also led her through another decade of trying to determine why her own historical understanding of the Black Panther Party (BPP) had been inaccurate. (She continued writing other books during this time, too.) She explained, "I became more angry about the way this history had been kept from me and is continuing to be kept from young readers today" ("Black Creators Series" 2021). The publication of her National Book Award finalist, *Revolution in Our Time: The Black Panther Party's Promise to the People* is a culmination of Magoon's commitment to her own process of reeducation and to her young readers to create a more accurate truth about a group that is often misunderstood and vilified.

With *The Rock and the River*, the book that announced her entry into the field of children's literature as the winner of the Coretta Scott King/John Steptoe Award, Magoon introduces several themes found in her body of work. The search for identity, the struggle to make the "right" decision, and the political, racialized milieu in which the main character, Sam, comes of age are the themes Magoon revisits consistently throughout her work. Magoon helps young readers understand historical happenings and ordinary young people who explore their identities and growing consciousness.

## THE ORDINARY AND EXTRAORDINARY IN HISTORY

*The Rock and the River* is a historical fiction middle-grade novel about the Black Panther Improvement Party and two brothers at odds with their father's commitment to nonviolence. The BPP occupies a particular space in the American imagination, while much about the group's community organizing receives lesser attention, especially in literature written for children and young adults. Magoon (2015) explains her deliberate focus on the Black Panthers as helping readers know all they did:

> The Panthers were controversial because a lot of people didn't understand their goals . . . I wrote these books in part to offer up the Panthers' side of the story

and to show how exciting their presence in the community was to young people who longed to make a difference and were tired of marching and protesting for change and being beaten down for their effort.

Through the main character, Sam, readers learn about the BPP's significant community work, valuing of education, and the importance of young people within the movement. Within that context, Sam learns his own power and the power of collective organizing. Magoon explains how these themes are ongoing, especially in her historical work. She says her books are all part of a "bigger picture of being someone who makes a difference, finds a way to use their voice, and connect with other people in service of a bigger picture" ("Black Creators," 2021). That someone is generally an ordinary individual who learns how extraordinary they can be.

Magoon also urges readers to rethink or reconsider their understanding of history. She places readers in situations that are detailed, compelling, and grounded in history. She is committed to an accurate retelling of history and centering the Black people responsible for creating change. Her commitment to "the unnamed people in the crowd" ("Kekla Magoon," 2009) encourages a range of readers to think they, too, are capable of taking the charge of youth activism for causes relevant to them.

Magoon seeks to also connect her readers to historical figures' younger selves. *X* (Magoon & Shabazz, 2016) is the story of Malcolm Little, the young man who later became Malcolm X. Cowritten with X's daughter, Ilyasah Shabazz, this historical fiction novel holds great potential for teachers of interdisciplinary subjects, especially those of ELA and social studies.

The decision to focus on Malcolm Little is exciting, as readers are able to consider how his formative years might have shaped the political activist Malcolm X became. Awarded numerous honors including an NAACP Image Award for Outstanding Literary Work for Youth/Teens, a Coretta Scott King Honor, a Walter Award, and a National Book Award Long-List selection, the novel is appropriate for whole-class novel study and inclusion in a classroom library for independent reading.

The intentional focus on Malcolm's adolescence encourages a connection to Malcolm's character and to universal themes. The book begins in 1945, with Malcolm Little hiding in a bathroom in New York, dreading a visit from numbers runner West Indian Archie over a dispute about a mistake Malcolm made. Prior to his dramatic moment of escape, Malcolm remarks, "I am Malcolm Little. I am my father's son. But to be my father's son means they will always come for me" (p. 5).

Malcolm's search for his identity propels the novel, especially as related to his father's legacy. For instance, Malcolm is deeply connected to his family, struggling to understand his father's murder, his mother's unsuccessful attempts to keep his family together, and the eventual separation from her and his siblings. As might be expected, these traumatic events impact him significantly.

Magoon and Shabazz also insist readers humanize Malcolm Little. Often, Malcolm talks about his feelings of loneliness, adrift as he floats from place to place. Magoon (2018) emphasizes this uncertainty as part of helping readers understand that Malcolm was not a hero, was not exceptional. She counters, "He had no idea what he would become, no idea of the full scope of his potential—and the ache of disappointment and self-doubt almost made him give up on everything" (p. 65).

Magoon continued that she hoped by reading about Malcolm's uncertainty and eventual transformation based on "small, positive changes in his life" young readers would also be inspired. "Who's to say many of the disillusioned young teens we encounter every day don't have similar potential within them? How can we inspire them to believe?" (p. 65). Magoon's emphasis on drawing parallels for today's young people so they can reach back into history and be inspired and reassured is commendable.

Teaching this novel allows educators to use historical fiction to build "historical empathy" (Barton & Levstik, 2009), described by the authors as a process where readers are "invite[d] to care with and about people in the past, to be concerned with what happened to them and how they experienced their lives" (pp. 207–208).

Because so much critical attention about Malcolm X can be decontextualized and even incorrect, *X* offers readers the opportunity to dig deeper into Malcolm Little's background amid a changing historical backdrop, while also understanding that Malcolm did not achieve success by himself. Rather, as Magoon (2018) contradicts, "If you read between the lines of any famous person's biography, you'll also find evidence of the family or friends or colleagues who supported that person" (p. 64). Readers, too, can extend an understanding for Malcolm Little as a young person trying to find his way.

## NUANCES IN CONTEMPORARY REALISTIC FICTION

Magoon mines the everyday for robust stories in her contemporary fiction. For example, the young adult novel *How It Went Down*, a 2015 Coretta Scott King Honor, tackles the killing of an unarmed Black boy through an alternative structure. Following the shooting of Tariq Johnson, an unarmed Black boy by a White shooter named Jack Franklin, the narrative is shared between the perspectives of eighteen different characters. Here, Magoon grapples with contemporary topics in a book deemed a "stark yet captivating read that is both relevant *and* necessary" (Thomas, 2014, emphasis in original).

Providing such a range of perspectives enables many readers to connect and process the story and what is ongoing in the world. Writing amid the continuous murders of unarmed Black men and boys by police, Magoon's narrative offers no simple solutions to who killed the young man at the novel's center. She contends:

> I wrote *How It Went Down* in response to the media coverage around the shooting deaths of young black men like Trayvon Martin and Michael Brown . . . The most interesting effects of controversy occur behind the headlines, so this novel explores how young people react in this kind of crisis, and how the shock and grief of loss might be compounded by the controversy and the national media attention. (Magoon & Lane, 2014)

Magoon does, indeed, take the reader behind the headlines, confronting "reality" from myriad perspectives that force readers to question the events of the murder, the impact and the lasting trauma on those close to the dead boy, and the similarities and distinctions between people and their daily realities. It is a focus and format she returns to in the follow-up novel, *Light It Up*. This time, the main character is a young Black girl killed by police violence, challenging readers to explore similar questions.

Equally important is Magoon's ability to craft thoughtful, complex characters. Whether it's a middle-school girl who struggles with seeing her own internal beauty in *Camo Girl*, or a high-achieving orphan missing her father and discovering her sexual identity in *37 Things I Love (in no particular order)*, Magoon explores the lives of her characters with tenderness and thought that enables a deeper exploration of their vulnerabilities. She channels the reality of her young readers' desires to belong, to be loved, and to be valued.

Ella, the protagonist of *Camo Girl,* has an unnamed skin condition, leaving the reader free to envision the character as they want and to empathize with the familiar angst of fitting in. Ella is friends with another boy, Zachariah ("Z"), in this middle-grade novel, and the two form a pair of outcasts that rely on each other. Magoon explains her reasoning for their friendship as follows: "I wrote about the highest form of friendship I could imagine—unconditional friendship—because I craved it back then and I still value and search for it now" (Smith, 2011).

She also includes themes of self-acceptance and fitting in, two themes she is personally connected to after experiencing her own struggles with them. Thus, while the search for identity is one many young readers can understand, Magoon weaves in messages about the importance of friendship and belonging, too, using the book as a model for broader discussions and under-standings about coming-of-age.

Magoon accepted the Boston Globe-Horn Book Award for Fiction and Poetry for the middle-grade novel *The Season of Styx Malone*. Her text lov-ingly captured the ways that Black children's ordinary lives can appeal to a broad audience. Magoon (2019) explained, "Our youth deserve many more love letters, not just reminders of their pain" (p. 55). *Styx Malone*'s is, indeed, an affirming testament to Blackness.

The three main characters, Black boys living in a small Indiana town, want lives that are extraordinary. They learn, however, that amid parental fears of racial violence and unstable family ties, the mundane nature of their friend-ship is the connective tissue. Because Magoon sees these characters as spe-cial and worthy, she imbues them with humor, age-appropriate drama, and a lasting respect for the importance of a loving community. Magoon surmised, "extraordinary is merely an extension of what is ordinary" (2019). As her writing demonstrates, there are powerful stories that can affirm, reflect, and inspire readers wherever they are.

## MAGOON'S ACTIVISM

Magoon has also challenged the publishing industry to become more diverse in representing Black and other audiences. She insists (2019), "Black chil-dren exist and they deserve to have stories told about themselves" (p. 53). She chafes at publishers' attempts to limit her creative work, especially about choosing to foreground books about Blackness that were not entirely about racism. Her resistance and determination to center Black experiences in her work, as well as advocating for that right for others, undergirds her work.

Magoon's understanding of Blackness and Black children is broad, deep, and robust. She refuses to have Blackness defined by White publishers who want her to center White heroes and White comfort. Magoon argues, "Overcoming racism is not all we are about, and it is not the only way we want to be seen" (p. 55). Extending her writing to include criticisms of the publishing industry and the whiteness of children's books publishing is Magoon's way of connecting her aim of reaching young readers with the broader goals of changing publishing.

Remarkably, Magoon considers neither her activism nor her success as singular. Citing the work of Mildred Taylor and Jacqueline Woodson as mentors, Magoon locates herself on a timeline that has been created by the work of Black women authors. She explains (2021), "I am a writer because I read Taylor's *and* Woodson's books. We represent three generations of Black women writing our truths, crafting our stories, making our observations about the world as it was, is, and could be" (p. 52, emphasis in original).

It is Magoon's respect for and love of these writers that inspire her and compel her to continue to make space for others. Her success is bound to a broader collective and the need to work diligently for spaces that enable Black writers, and others, to flourish.

## CLASSROOM ACTIVITIES

Educators have many possibilities to incorporate Magoon's texts in their classrooms. All of her texts should be included in classroom libraries. Her middle-grade novels are excellent for *self-selected book clubs*. Teachers might group them around themes (i.e., friendship, family, overcoming challenges) and encourage students to choose a book that resonates with their interests. See the work of Cherry-Paul and Johansen (2019) for specifics about incorporating book clubs.

Magoon's *Revolution in Our Time: The Black Panther Party's Promise to the People* provides an excellent *whole-class* opportunity for students to challenge what they don't know about history. Taking the time to carefully create a setting that encourages respectful discussion, especially about race and racism (see Let's Talk! By Teaching for Tolerance), teachers and students can draw on the Black Historical Consciousness Principles (King, 2020) as they work through the book.

Using a multidisciplinary study of the book's content, students can analyze images, quotations, individuals, and actions to explore a more accurate and nuanced understanding of the work of the Black Panther movement. They can use internet sources and archives to do the work of historians: (1) generate an essential question of their own from the text, (2) select pieces of evidence from *Revolution* to support their thinking, and (3) connect their understanding to the present.

Throughout the novel study, educators can help students contextualize the work of the Black Panthers with similar movements and the work of young people in creating change. The unit can conclude with students thinking through, and presenting in a format of their choice, a problem of interest to them and a solution.

Finally, educators can incorporate any of Magoon's work into a *study of writing craft,* especially for sentence study. For instance, teachers can ask students what they notice about Magoon's word choice, imagery, etc., as they guide students through writing their own sentences based on Magoon's mentor one. Then, students can try their hand at writing in a similar style as they draft their own work.

## CONCLUSION

Kekla Magoon adeptly captures the range of Blackness for her young readers through a thoughtful, loving centering of everyday characters. She focuses on the unknown, often-overlooked voices in history and the present, knowing that those characters have important stories to tell. Her desire to unearth the unknown or inaccurate histories also lets Black and other readers understand that they matter and that their presence is vital.

As Magoon continues to expand narratives of Blackness and push the publishing industry to center all kinds of stories about Black children in an expansive way, she demands we pay careful attention to the ways that the ordinary stories illuminate the extraordinary lives her characters lead and that we are invited to share.

## PRIMARY WORKS

Magoon, K. (2010). *The Rock and the River*. Aladdin.
Magoon, K. (2011). *Today the World Is Watching You: The Little Rock Nine and the Fight for School Integration*. Twenty-First Century Books.
Magoon, K. (2012). *Camo Girl*. Aladdin.
Magoon, K. (2013). *Fire in the Streets*. Aladdin.
Magoon, K. (2013). *37 Things I Love (In No Particular Order)*. Square Fish.
Magoon, K. (2015). *How It Went Down*. Square Fish.
Magoon, K. (2016). *Shadows of Sherwood*. Bloomsbury.
Magoon, K. & Shabazz, I. (2016). *X*. Candlewick.
Magoon, K. (2017). *A Rebellion of Thieves*. Bloomsbury.
Magoon, K. (2017). *A Reign of Outlaws*. Bloomsbury.
Magoon, K. (2018). *The Season of Styx Malone*. Wendy Lamb.
Magoon, K. (2019). *Light It Up*. Henry Holt & Co.
Magoon, K. (2021). *The Flag Never Touched the Ground: America's Brave Black Regiment in Battle*. Pushkin.
Magoon, K. & Freeman, L. (2021). *The Highest Tribute: Thurgood Marshall's Life, Leadership, and Legacy*. Quill Tree Books.
Magoon, K. (2021). *She Persisted: Ruby Bridges*. Philomel.
Magoon, K. (2021). *Revolution in Our Time: The Black Panther Party's Promise to the People*. Candlewick.

## REFERENCES

Barton, K. C., & Levstik, L. S. (2009). *Teaching History for the Common Good*. New York: Routledge, Taylor & Francis.

Black Creators. (Nov. 16, 2021). Series 2, Episode 1, Kekla Magoon. [Facebook Page]. Retrieved November 26, 2021, from https://www.facebook.com/reading andwritingproject/videos/2889692684674534/?__so__=channel_tab&__rv__=latest_videos_card.

Kekla Magoon. (2010, February 03). Retrieved from https://thebrownbookshelf.com /2010/02/03/kekla-magoon/

Kekla Magoon (2015, August 19). Writing Historical Fiction. Retrieved from http:// www.bookologymagazine.com/article/6359

Magoon, K. (2018, May). The Un-Hero's Journey. *Horn Book Magazine, XCIV*(3), 62–65.

National Writing Project. (n.d.). Retrieved from https://www.nwp.org/cs/public/print /resource/4266

Thomas, E. E. (2014, October 30). A black teen is shot in Kekla Magoon's "How It Went Down". Retrieved from http://www.latimes.com/books/jacketcopy/la-ca-jc -kekla-magoon-20141102-story.html

## SCHOLARLY WORKS

Bird, B. (2009, February 11). Review of the Day: The Rock and the River by Kekla Magoon. Retrieved from http://blogs.slj.com/afuse8production/2009/02/11/review -of-the-day-the-rock-and-the-river-by-kekla-magoon/

Magoon, K. (May/June 2019). A vision for the CSK: Past, present and future. *The Horn Book Magazine*, pp. 51–55.

Magoon, K. (January/February 2020). Fiction and poetry award winner. *The Horn Book Magazine,* pp. 32–35.

Magoon, K. (July/August 2021). Our foundation, our springboard: The trailblazing work of Mildred D. Taylor and Jacqueline Woodson. *The Horn Book Magazine*, pp. 50–53.

## CLASSROOM ACTIVITIES

Cherry-Paul, S. & Johansen, D. (2019). *Breathing New Life into Book Clubs: A Practical Guide for Teachers*. Heinemann.

King, L. (2020). Black history is not American history: Toward a framework of Black historical consciousness. *Social Education 84*(6), pp. 335–341.

Teaching Tolerance. (2019). *Let's Talk: A Guide to Facilitating Critical Conversations With Students*. Montgomery: The Southern Poverty Law Center.

## AUTHOR NOTE

Correspondence concerning this chapter should be addressed to Kimberly Parker. Email: kimpossible97@gmail.com

*Chapter 6*

# Jason Reynolds

## The Boy in the Black Suit *and the Struggle with Grief*

### Dani Rimbach-Jones and Steven T. Bickmore

"We are living in the era of Jason Reynolds."

—Meg Medina (2019 UNLV Summit)

Saying Jason Reynolds is the next Walter Dean Myers might be an understatement. This should not be taken as a statement to minimize either author or the other authors in this book or this series. Comparisons of this kind might allow us to forget the impact of the forerunner and dismiss the individual efforts and prowess of the next generation. Yet with the announcement of Reynolds as the 2020–2021 Youth Ambassador for the Library of Congress, is shining a light on his talent and acknowledging the influence he has on young readers.

Since, *When I was the Greatest* (2014), Reynolds has carved his own path. The publishing world and the critics have embraced him—praising his work and his efforts to advocate for literacy activities that engage adolescents. At the age of thirty-five Reynolds was nominated back to back in 2016 and 2017 for the National Book Award (NBA): *A Long Way Down* (2016) and *Ghost* (2017); then he hit the 2019 shortlist with *Look Both Ways* (2019). The impact of his work with Brendan Kiely, *All American Boys*, is tremendous. His foray into the verse novel with *Long Way Down* and its allusions to *A Christmas Carol* is significant.

Jason Reynolds walks the path of other African-American authors before him, but he is also carving a new one for himself and future generations. With the publication of *Stamped* (2020), Reynolds is recognized for writing young adult (YA) literature that addresses racism as a social and systemic structure. Reynolds's work with Dr. Ibram X. Kendi received critical reception for its attention to details that point out the racist ideologies embedded in systems and structures within the United States, but also provides a guide for readers to help eliminate racist structures they encounter. They have also adapted *Stamped* for children as well—*Stamped: For Kids* (2021).

## CRITICAL RECEPTION AND FUTURE PROMISE

An examination of the history of the NBA over the first twenty years reveals a noticeable lack of diverse authors (Bickmore, Infante-Sheridan, and Ying, 2017). Some early winners were diverse, but the number of winners and nominees does not approach the representative statistics of the country's diverse population over the same time period. The need for an organization and a movement like #WeNeedDiverseBooks is evident. More is being done and diverse authors are making it to both the long list and the shortlist of the NBA and other YA book awards.

It is important to note that while Jason has and continues to receive literary acclaim, he is not alone. The last five to ten years have been a windfall of African-American authors. Many of the other ten authors in this volume published their first novel within the last five years. Others have been working steadily for a decade or more as their readership has grown and the awards have begun to arrive. In addition, the works they are writing represent a range of genres from graphic novels, suspense fiction, adventure novels, psychological thrillers, speculative fiction, middle-grade books, and novels in verse.

As the book is prepared for publication, it is easy to name other African-American authors that could have easily been included in this book. This might include Brandy Colbert, Brittany Morris, Bethany Morris, Kwame Mbalia, Nic Stone, Angie Thomas, Dhonielle Clayton, Jay Coles, and Nicola Yoon, among many others. While the authors are becoming more numerous, it is important to note that diverse students need to see these books, in classrooms and libraries. They need them in their hands and the goals of the Brown Bookshelf and We Need Diverse books should be addressed by librarians, teachers, authors, and reading activists.

## DISCUSSION OF *THE BOY IN THE BLACK SUIT*

With the death of Matt's mother, the family structure that exemplified his childhood and adolescent years ceases to exist. Coming home after school to two happily married parents is in the past. Reynold does an astounding job of examining death and loss on an individual level, familial level, and within a community. He presents an examination of the importance of matriarchy in African-American culture. Reynold paints the essence of Matt's mother, Daisy's soul on every single page of the novel; thus, showing his reader that even though loved one's may no longer be with them, their memory and impact remain.

Her death drives Matt's and Jackson's character development: Matt's development is apparent through his work at the funeral home with Mr. Ray, his refusal to cook a meal, his continuous listening to Tupac's *Dear Mama*, and his budding relationship with Lovey. Matt's growth is positive—moving him toward a direction of who he might want to be in the future.

On the other hand, Jackson relapses to drinking, hanging out with Mr. Ray's "no good brother," Cork, and then, recovering from a horrific accident that incapacitates him. Jackson has to struggle to not become the person he once was prior to his marriage to Daisy. These sequences of events for both characters occur in large part due to their individual responses to losing a mother and a wife.

Matt, at first, refuses to work at Mr. Ray's funeral home. He does not wish to be at the place that reminds him of the worst day of his life. "But on the other hand, it just did not seem like a good idea to take a job somewhere where I'd have to relive my mom's funeral every day" (Reynolds, 2015, p. 13). This thought does not last long; Matt changes his mind and hesitantly accepts Mr. Ray's offer to work at his funeral home.

As Matt begins working for Mr. Ray, Matt begins to wear his black suit every day (the same one he wore to his mother's funeral) and attends funerals. He felt the need to watch and witness—to know if others are feeling what he "had been feeling." This pattern continues; watching others wail, cry, and mourn.

The two, Mr. Ray and Matt, begin to develop a close relationship—one that is of significance to Matt in realizing that he is not the only one who has lost someone or something. Matt slowly becomes Mr. Ray's right-hand man. Mr. Ray is picking Matt up after school, feeding him, and ensuring he gets home safe. When Jackson is in a car accident, Mr. Ray becomes the pivotal figure that Matt needed. Someone to be there when he feared he would lose another parent and someone to show him that he is not alone in grief either.

Mr. Ray becomes "maybe more like an uncle" (Reynolds 2015, p. 110) as Matt describes—Mr. Ray worries and ensures that Matt matters. To let him know that he is not forsaken and that he is understood. Shortly after Jackson's car accident, Mr. Ray shows Matt his "my pain room. My vault" (Reynold 2015, p. 105). In there, Matt sees newspaper clippings of Mr. Ray's college basketball career and the one clip that reads "William Ray, Broken Knee; Shining Star's Season Over" (Reynolds 2015, p. 103)—the end of his basketball career. Matt also learns in his time down in Mr. Ray's vault that he even lost his wife, Ella, at the age of twenty-nine.

Matt questions why Mr. Ray is sharing this with him. To Mr. Ray's response: "I guess I've been waiting to show someone who would . . . get it" (Reynolds 2015, p. 105). No other words are spoken—it actually jumps to playing I-DEE-clare-war. But the moment of silence between the two symbolizes their understanding and empathy of one another.

During Matt's time working at Mr. Ray's funeral home, he meets Lovey— at her grandmother's funeral. But Lovey differs from Matt—she takes loss and sadness with stride. That is the complete opposite of Matt, but their differing views of loss begin their relationship. Matt wants to know "What made her so strong. What made her so different" (Reynolds 2015, p. 130) and how for Lovey "it definitely got easier" (Reynolds 2015, p. 138).

Lovey didn't lose her mom to cancer, a heart attack, or anything of that nature. Love's mother, Renee Brown, was snatched from this world—she was murdered. Ten years prior, on a Valentine's Day, Lovey's mother was murdered by a man who thought she was cheating. This all occurred in Building 516—the same building Chris grew up in. The same building where Matt had a sleepover that he recalled from his memory (pg. 44–45).

One of the most sophisticated aspects of this novel is that Reynolds leaves the problems unresolved. The future is uncertain, but he leaves us with a character, Matt, who is immersed in hope, or at least in actions and choices that indicates his grief did not consume him, but changed him, taught him, and contributed to his growth as a young man. As the title of the last chapter states, life is taken one step at a time and now, at least, he is taking steps through another funeral, another moment and marker of grief with his fingers entwined with another human. Together they ease their own and each other's grief. They are Sempervivum.

## DEATH IS EVERYWHERE—CLASSROOM ACTIVITIES OR INSTRUCTIONAL FOCUS

When we were originally looking at the development of classroom activities, the chapter authors Steve and Dani live in Las Vegas and cannot ignore how deeply the Route 91 Harvest Festival Shooting in Las Vegas, Nevada, affected our community. As a result, they wanted to provide a structure for teachers to facilitate those discussions about community loss in the classroom. However, upon collaboration and considering the drastic upheaving of COVID-19, they decided to explore how teachers might discuss the losses that communities felt and are continuing to feel as a result of this pandemic.

The ripple effect of COVID-19 is not over and for many this is still a raw wound that is healing, but youth need to have a safe place to discuss how their lives were turned upside down and might not ever be the same again.

The year 2020 has been tumultuous; many people, adolescents and children included, lost their lives that we were living pre-COVID, some even lost their loved ones to the virus, and some of us even lost who we were. And, sadly many of these tragedies have continued throughout 2021.

This was the first time many of us as adults and for a majority of our students were seeing and dealing with loss and death on a daily basis. There was no hiding from it—the news kept reporting on the increase of infected people, it was evident on the empty grocery shelves, we were even seeing loss of lives in Black Lives Matter protest. Death was and is everywhere—seeming to swallow us up whole at any moment. Therefore, this is why we are encouraging educators to bring the topic of death into their classroom; to support our youth in dealing with loss and keeping hope for their futures.

Nonetheless, nearly every canonical text taught in the ELA classroom contains a death of at least one character. If we look at *Romeo and Juliet*, it is double suicide that could have been prevented. *Hamlet*, there is murder. Death is central in *Of Mice of Men, Things Fall Apart, Frankenstein, Their Eyes Were Watching God, To Kill a Mockingbird*, and the list goes on and on. Not once in any pedagogical approach have educators taught these books in their approach to death.

Pushing aside the cannon that is being taught in school and the lack of acknowledgment of death, even popular YAL such as *Harry Potter, Hunger Games, Divergent, The Hate U Give*, and *Dear Martin* all deal with death in one way or another. This then leads to the following questions, why do we ignore death in the K-12 classroom? Or why do we only acknowledge death when it is at the expense of Black bodies being murdered?

In the current world that our students are living in they are seeing death in every corner—the media with the murders being done to Black bodies, suicide, and death from COVID-19. It is imperative that books, such as *The Boy in the Black Suit*, are available for our adolescents. It is as Mr. Ray puts it "And I realized that it's not that death is bad. It's not" (Reynolds 2015, p. 245).

We as educators need to be guiding our students to see that death is not only a bleak ending, where everything fades to darkness. We are all going to die, but what we should be doing and teaching our youth is how to get the most out of their lives. Asking them to think about what trail they want to pave for future generations. Therefore, it is imperative that we, educators, provide a plethora of tools for our students to grapple with death and, even more importantly, find hope during the lives that they are living.

Asking students to talk about grief and loss is asking young adults to share some of the most vulnerable parts of themselves. An example of this is seen in the character Mr. Ray. His ability to share with Matt and provide a model of living beyond grief is important. This character relationship is a monumental example for your readers. With the following activities and in many other activities, students should be controlling and designing the activities, assessments, and end goals with the guidance of a teacher.

## ACTIVITY 1: PRE-READING ACTIVITY (MY GRIEF)

Grief and loss do not just have to be dealing with death and never seeing a loved one again. Grief and loss could be dealing with the loss of an identity or something personal. The reader is able to witness this when Mr. Ray, who Matt confides in deeply, states how he deals with the loss of his basketball career and his wife. A good part of Mr. Ray's identity was wrapped up in being a college star basketball player and a husband; when he could no longer play he had to grieve that loss.

Later, his wife's death produces another level of grief and its resulting effects. Reynolds is not saying losing a career is the same as Matt losing his mother to cancer, but Reynolds strategically includes loss of identity, ensuring that all readers have the potential to relate at different levels. It also might be the first step for them to begin to feel comfortable discussing such personal issues. As students begin talking about loss and grief, it is important to remind them that they need not share anything personal that would make them uncomfortable. In fact, they should feel comfortable creating a scenario of some kind of loss for a fictional character.

Materials needed for the "Wall of Grief and Loss":

- Poster paper/classroom wall
- Small pieces of paper/sticky note
- Tape/glue
- Big bowl

### Step 1:

Place a giant poster on one of the walls of your classroom. Title it the "Wall of Grief and Loss." Give each student a piece of paper or a sticky note. Inform them to NOT write their name on the paper. On the paper or the sticky note, have each of the students identify one to two things that they lost during COVID—they identify a loss of identity, what changed in their lives, etc. Once they are done, have the students fold up their paper and place it in the big bowl. When all the students have finished, take each one of the pieces of paper and glue it or tape it to the "Wall of Grief and Loss."

## Step 2:

Have the students take a moment and go and observe the "Wall of Grief and Loss." During their observations, have the students identify two commonalities they are seeing on the "Wall of Grief and Loss."

## Optional Step 3:

For Step 3, there are three options for your students to discuss the common findings of the "Wall of Grief and Loss." You, as an educator, know your students and how they will best react, and which options might be best for their success.

*Option 1:* Have the students share out to the class what commonalities they concluded from the "Wall of Grief and Loss."
*Option 2:* Have the students write an exit ticket discussing what commonalities they found and why they identify those commonalities in particular.
*Option 3:* Have the students find a partner and discuss the commonalities that they both identified.

The teacher can build on this activity when the students return to class. They can form small groups and investigate resources that might help people who are struggling with loss or grief. Doing this as a group provides a level of community comfort for students who may feel isolated or who may be experiencing a level of loss or grief themselves. The teacher might collect a list of resources (see textbox 6.1) or, depending on the expertise of the students, allow them to find their own sites.

### TEXTBOX 6.1

### Grief Support

- Dougy Center Teen Resource
- Teenage Grief Sucks
- Actively Moving Forward
- What's Your Grief
- The Dinner Party

In order to build other communication skills, each group can also be required to create an infographic or a poster that can serve as an advertisement for the organization they have investigated. Once completed, each group should present their product to the whole class. After each group has presented their product, the teacher might organize an anonymous vote to see which product the class feels most effectively represents its organization.

## ACTIVITY 2: DURING READING (OUR GRIEF OR THE GRIEF OF OTHERS)

Often, teachers spend a great deal of time introducing a novel and then discussing the novel as a whole once the students have completed the reading. However, the time a student spends during a novel is significant. It is helpful to provide opportunities for students to consider the plot, the characters, and the themes as they develop throughout the course of reading the novel.

When reading *The Boy in The Black Suit* as a class, identify what Mr. Ray, Matt, and Lovey do to get through their grief. Next, have your students explain a possible reason as to why the character does what they do. We recommend that you fill this out as a class and have them labeled on the whiteboard or on large pieces of paper hanging around the classroom.

For example:

Mr. Ray:

1.  "Pain room, vault" → Mr. Ray might do this to keep his grief locked away, that way it does not consume him.
2.  Keeps newspaper clippings → Mr. Ray does this so that he can at least remember his college basketball career versus erasing any trace of it.
3.  Keep the photo of his wife → This way Mr. Ray can remember his wife and the memories they shared.

Here are some examples of guiding questions to analyze Mr. Ray: Why does Mr. Ray keep all the newspaper clippings and the photo of his deceased wife solely in his vault? Why does he not have wedding photos of her around his house possibly? (These questions can be used in a Socratic discussion or for personal writing.)

Matthew Miller

1.  Replays the song "Dear Mama" by 2Pac → Matt states he plays this song to drown out his thoughts. He also states that it is like 2Pac singing a lullaby just for him.
2.  Goes to funerals → Matt states consistently throughout the novel that he goes to funerals to see that moment when people are about to break. It lets him know that he is not alone.

Here are some examples of guiding questions to analyze Matt (Give the students a copy of the lyrics "Dear Mama"): After reading the 2Pac's lyrics, what are some potential reasons as to why Matt feels this is a lullaby just for him? What are your thoughts about Matt attending funerals of people he does not know? Would you do the same if you were in his shoes? (These questions can be used in a Socratic discussion or for personal writing.)

Lovey:

1. She takes photos → Lovey's grandma taught her to take photos to hold onto the memories.

Here are some examples of guiding questions to analyze Lovey: Why might taking photos help a person grieve? Mr. Ray locks his photos in his "vault" and Lovey takes them and surrounds herself with them, explore the possibilities of their different approaches to photographs. (These questions can be used in a Socratic discussion or for personal writing.)

This series of activities and questions can provide students with guidance as they read the text and think about the grief that others in their community or circle of friends are dealing with. Even more importantly, some of the students might be dealing with their own levels of grief. If such is the case, and this information becomes obvious to the teacher, the teacher might chat with the student and make their situation known to the school counselor or other individuals who can provide adequate counsel.

## ACTIVITY 3: AFTER READING (MOVING FROM GRIEF TO LEAVING A LEGACY)

In the kitchen of Matt's home, there is a cookbook his mother left for him, *The Secret for Getting Girls, for Matty*. There was advice in there from his mom to help him move things forward with Lovey. That is what your classroom cookbook is going to do for your students. There will actually be recipes in there for the students to share from their culture or have a special meaning to them. There are four components that should be included on their recipe page:

1. Ingredients—The students should have a list of ingredients others will need if they wish to replicate the recipe.
2. Directions—There should be a step-by-step process that walks a person through on how to make the dish.
3. Sage Advice—Your students should write a little snippet of sage advice or wisdom. This advice IS NOT about the recipe itself. It is about life, school, relationships, whatever advice they want to offer.
4. Get Creative—Allow your students to be creative. Give them the space to add funny lines about making the recipe, draw, color, etc. The teacher can make sure that students are familiar with such programs as Adobe Spark and Canva. (See figure 6.1, for example.)

**Figure 6.1 Recipe Example.** *Source:* Author Created via canva author - Dani Rimbach-jone.

As an educator, have a binder that keeps this collection, allow it to become a generational token where students past, present and future, may look at for advice. Another option is to create a google folder that the class shares. Some teachers might have the ability to share community work through a feature on a class webpage or grading application.

## CONCLUSION

Death is a part of every day life; and yes, it can be scary because not a single one of us knows what we face when our time here is done on Earth. Nonetheless, Jason Reynold's *The Boy in the Black Suit* presents the readers with multiple characters dealing and coping with grief in multiple ways. The reader walks alongside Matt as he sits through funerals—allowing him to see he is not alone in his grief. Then there is Mr. Ray who locks his grief in a vault and lastly, there is Lovey, who refuses to be sad. Each of these characters has the potential to reach a student and help them through their grief.

If 2020 and 2021 have taught us anything, it is that no one is able to avoid death. Not just death itself, those who live in the wake of losing a loved one must find a way to accept the loss and move on with their lives. *The Boy in the Black Suit* does just that, Reynolds teaches his reader that they must work through grief in a way that allows them to live happy and productive lives— to not die with the ones we love.

## SELECTED BIBLIOGRAPHY

Petry, A., & Reynolds, J. (2018). *Harriet Tubman: conductor on the Underground Railroad* (Revised edition. ed.). New York: Amistad, an imprint of HarperCollins Publishers.

Reynolds, J. (2014). *When I was the greatest* (First edition. ed.). New York: Atheneum Books for Young Readers.

Reynolds, J. (2015). *The boy in the black suit* (First edition. ed.). New York: Atheneum Books for Young Readers.

Reynolds, J. (2016a). *As brave as you* (First Edition. ed.). New York: Atheneum Books for Young Readers.

Reynolds, J. (2016b). *Ghost* (First Edition. ed.). New York: Atheneum Books For Young Readers.

Reynolds, J. (2017a). *Long way down* (First edition. ed.). New York: Atheneum.

Reynolds, J. (2017b). *Miles Morales, Spider-Man* (First edition. ed.). Los Angeles; New York: Marvel.

Reynolds, J. (2017c). *Patina* (First edition. ed.). New York: Atheneum Books for Young Readers.

Reynolds, J. (2018a). *For every one* (First edition. ed.). New York: Atheneum.

Reynolds, J. (2018b). *Lu* (First edition. ed.). New York: Atheneum.

Reynolds, J. (2018c). *Sunny* (First edition. ed.). New York: Atheneum Books for Young Readers.

Reynolds, J., & Griffin, J. (2009). *My name is Jason. Mine too: our story, our way* (1st ed.). New York: Joanna Citler Books.

Reynolds, J., & Kiely, B. (2015). *All American boys* (1st ed.). New York: Atheneum Books for Young Readers.

Reynolds, J., & Nabaum, A. (2019). *Look both ways: a tale told in ten blocks*. New York: Atheneum/Caitlyn Dlouhy Books.

Zoboi, I. A., Watson, R. e., Johnson, V., Henderson, L., Giles, L. R., Magoon, K., . . . (2019). *Black enough: stories of being young & black in America* (1st ed.). New York: Balzer + Bray, an imprint of HarperCollins Publishers.

## REFERENCES

Bickmore, S. T., Xu, Y., & Sheridan, M. I. (2017). Where Are the People of Color?: Representation of Cultural Diversity in the National Book Award for Young People's Literature and Advocating for Diverse Books in a Non-Post Racial Society. *Taboo: The Journal of Culture and Education, 16*(1). doi:10.31390/taboo.16.1.06

Medina, Meg. "Developing Clave". 2019 UNLV Summit on the Research and Teaching of Young Adult Literature, College of Education at the University of Nevada, Las Vegas. Las Vegas, NV. May 30, 2019.

*Chapter 7*

# Varian Johnson

## *Discovering the Mysteries of Our Past through* The Parker Inheritance

### Alex Corbitt

Varian Johnson's contributions to young adult (YA) literature span an array of genres and audiences. His early novels (*Saving Maddie, My Life as A Rhombus*, and *Red Polka Dot in a World of Plaid*) cater to older readers and grapple with morally thorny themes. His contemporary works connect with younger audiences and range from fantasy (*The Return* or The *Wildcat's Claw*), to realistic fiction (*The Great Greene Heist* or *To Catch a Cheat*), to mystery and historical fiction (*The Parker Inheritance*).

Johnson is both critically acclaimed and prolific. Notably, *The Great Greene Heist* was named a Kirkus Reviews Best Book, an ALA Notable Children's Book, and a Texas Library Association Lone Star List selection. *To Catch a Cheat* was featured on the Kids' Indie Next List. In addition, *The Parker Inheritance* won the Coretta Scott King Author Honor and the Boston Globe-Horn Book Honor Award.

Beyond his awards and distinction, Johnson is a founding member of The Brown Bookshelf—a blog spotlighting Black writers and their work for young readers. Johnson situates himself as an advocate for Black representation in literature. Perhaps his most significant contribution is his ability to craft complex narratives that explore many Black experiences. This is exemplified in his novel *The Parker Inheritance*.

### THE PARKER INHERITANCE

*The Parker Inheritance*, at surface level, is a mystery novel about two kids searching for a hidden fortune. Twelve-year-old Candice Miller has recently moved to Lambert, South Carolina, in the wake of her parents' divorce. She and her mother live in the house of the late Abigail Caldwell, Candice's maternal grandmother. Candice and her new neighborhood friend, Brandon Jones, discover an old, cryptic letter to Abigail. The letter outlines clues to a multimillion dollar reward for the person who can piece together Lambert's hidden history of racial injustice.

Johnson draws direct parallels between *The Parker Inheritance* and Ellen Raskin's classic mystery, *The Westing Game*. In interviews, Johnson shares his admiration for Raskin and says he reads *The Westing Game* once a year. Like Johnson, Candice and Brandon find inspiration from *The Westing Game* as they read it throughout their adventure. Capturing the riddle and wonder of *The Westing Game* was at the forefront of Johnson's creative process.

*The Parker Inheritance* features a merging of Johnson's narrative writing styles. The mystery elements of the story mirror the playfulness of Johnson's recent works, while the historical fiction elements of the story reflect the mature, challenging themes of Johnson's early works. As Candice and Brandon dig deeper into their treasure hunt, they uncover Lambert's hidden history of racism, violence, and injustice.

The kids' research reveals the story of Lambert, South Carolina, in the late 1950s. After the *Brown v. Board of Education* ruling, Lambert's public schools resisted integration. Members of the Black community debated the need for integration. A character named Leanne Washington argued that progress is incremental and dreamed of a day when Black students could attend integrated, equal-opportunity schools. Leanne's husband, Enoch, believed that the Black community already thrived without white folks. He warned Leanne that Black teachers would lose their jobs in the process of integration.

Johnson writes Lambert's historical scenes as flashbacks throughout the novel. The characters' dialogue poses readers with moral quandaries that resist easy answers. Johnson's style is never preachy. Instead, his prose seems to respect the criticality of young readers and engage them with social issues that our society continues to wrestle with today. To this end, readers have the opportunity to investigate Lambert's history alongside Candice and Brandon.

As Lambert's history is excavated through flashbacks and the kids' research, we learn of Reginald Bradley and Siobhan Washington. Reginald Bradley was the star tennis player for Perkins High School, the town's school for Black students. Siobhan was the intelligent daughter of Enoch Washington (Reginald's tennis coach). Reginald and Siobhan were secretly in love, but their relationship was fractured when a tennis game between Perkins High School and Wallace High School (the town's school for white students) resulted in racially motivated violence. As a result, Enoch was severely wounded, and Reginald narrowly fled Lambert.

Reginald had very light skin. Under problematic counsel, the exiled Reginald decided to reinvent himself as a white man named James Parker. Reginald, now James Parker, went on to become an astoundingly wealthy businessman. Though monetarily successful, Reginald had completely renounced his true identity. When Reginald returned to Lambert decades later, Siobhan objected to his masquerade.

Siobhan argued that Reginald's proximity to whiteness had ruined his character. Reginald hesitated to date Black women, condoned racist jokes in the workplace, failed to hire Black employees at his company, and even devastated Lambert's Black community in his quest for revenge against old enemies. Sobered by Siobhan's feedback, Reginald worked to remedy his transgressions, restore Lambert, and shed James Parker. He is revealed to be the benefactor of the mysterious fortune Candice and Brandon are hunting.

Varian Johnson interrogates the persistence of racism by juxtaposing the racism of 1950s Lambert with the racism of modern-day Lambert. In one haunting scene, Candice and Brandon are confronted by Assistant Principal Rittenhauer while conducting research at Lambert High School. Mr. Rittenhauer assumes they are stealing something and threatens to frisk them. However, when another faculty member confirms that Candice and Brandon are conducting research, Mr. Rittenhauer writes off the encounter as a "misunderstanding." This exchange highlights how racism is veiled in modern contexts.

In addition to racism, *The Parker Inheritance* also addresses issues of sexism and homophobia. For example, Brandon doesn't like to read "girl" books and insults a townswoman by calling her "the type of woman" who is too weak to divorce her unfaithful husband. Brandon's grandfather also exhibits ugly prejudices when shaming Brandon for being gay. Candice challenges Brandon's misogyny and his grandfather's homophobia throughout the novel. She often repeats the phrase, "We hear what we want to hear. We see what we want to see," as a reminder that our biases can distort our thinking and relationships with others.

*The Parker Inheritance* is a novel of incredible scope and craft. Johnson uses YA literature to center the genius of Black characters, interrogate modern and historical racism, and provoke justice-oriented conversations that intersect across issues of race, gender, and sexuality. Thus, the text offers teachers and students a wealth of opportunities for critical discourse and learning.

## TEACHING *THE PARKER INHERITANCE*

The thematic and narrative layers of *The Parker Inheritance* are ripe for inquiry and investigation at the small group and whole-class level. Below are two classroom activities informed by the NCTE/IRA Standards for the ELA.

## Small-Group Discussion: Sustaining Racial
## Identities through Difference

*The Parker Inheritance* raises many questions about identity, community, and white privilege. For example, Reginald Bradley, a light-skinned Black man, pretended to be White after fleeing Lambert. While this plan yielded Reginald aspects of White privilege, Siobhan Washington confronted him and argued that he had turned his back on the Black community. The confrontation served as the impetus for Reginald to repent and change his ways. Reginald's story can be paired with various other texts to promote students' critical inquiry into concepts of whiteness, assimilation, and difference.

In the Author's Note, Johnson cites various people in history who were multiracial but passed as White: an entertainer named Ina Ray Hutton, a comic writer named George Herriman, and a *New York Times* critic named Anatole Broyard. Students can research these historical figures in small groups and discuss how their stories compare to Reginald's story. These discussions can be an entry point into creating extended definitions of "white privilege" and critiquing how whiteness is centered in media and society.

Brit Bennett's novel *The Vanishing Half* (2020) is another portrayal of how Black characters situate their identities relative to whiteness. Like Reginald, the sisters in Bennett's novel (Stella and Desiree Vignes) are light-skinned Black characters. Whereas Stella endeavors to integrate into White society, Desiree sustains her identity by embracing her Black heritage. This novel, paired with *The Parker Inheritance*, highlights how racial identity can be diminished through assimilation and sustained through difference.

To understand how Reginald's story in a modern context, students can also read and discuss Ta-Nehisi Coates's article, "I'm Not Black, I'm Kanye" (2018). Coates's essay critiques Kanye West's endorsement of the 45th president of the United States. The piece details the political implications of Kanye's actions and how his endorsement worked to legitimize destructive policing, deportation, voter suppression, and attacks on reproductive justice. Like Siobhan, Coates argues that Black people in positions of power have an increased responsibility to represent their communities.

During classroom conversations about sustaining racial identity through difference, students can learn how white culture has historically appropriated Black culture. PBS Teachers' Lounge writer, Ray Yang (2019), wrote a blog article titled "Cultural Appropriation: What's An Educator's Role?" that provides teachers with resources to discuss this issue with youth. By foregrounding the joy and genius of Black culture, educators can help students rethink cultural practices of assimilation and appropriation that reify whiteness under the guise of "sameness."

The above series of small-group conversations connect with NCTE/IRA Standard 11. Standard 11 reads: *Students participate as knowledgeable, reflective, creative, and critical members of a variety of literacy communities.* Through intertextual inquiry and discourse, students can work together to explore complex issues of race, identity, and belonging.

## Whole-Class Project: The Memorial Room

When Candice and Brandon conducted research at Lambert High School, a history teacher took them into the Memorial Room—a museum space that paid tribute to Lambert's history. When exploring this room, the kids discovered antiques that celebrated Lambert's Black community. One such item was a 1950s trophy that commemorated Lambert's Black tennis team's victory over its White team. Emulating the Memorial Room, students can work together to transform their classroom space into a museum that centers and celebrates Black history in the United States.

Candice and Brandon demonstrate how researching the histories of our town, state, and country requires us to confront our nation's history of colonization and racial oppression. To help students conduct critical research about Black life in the United States, it is important to provide them with resources that acknowledge how Black culture has thrived despite systemic injustices. Organizations like Facing History and Ourselves and The Zinn Education Project provide free, critical readings and historical artifacts for readers of all ages. Blackpast.org is another excellent resource for researching Black historical figures and landmarks by state.

After collecting historical documents and artifacts on Black history, students can collaborate to turn their classroom into a Memorial Room. This process entails curatorial conversations about how the pieces are arranged by subject, period, and theme. Upon organizing the artifacts around the room, each student can select an exhibit and write a curator's description. This description can describe the artifact, explain how it highlights an element of Black culture in the United States, and reflect on how their research process compared to Candice and Brandon's experience.

The research components of the Memorial Room project reflect NCTE/IRA Standard 7. Standard 7 reads: *Students conduct research on issues and interests by generating ideas and questions and by posing problems. They gather, evaluate, and synthesize data from a variety of sources to communicate their discoveries in ways that suit their purpose and audience.* Pairing *The Parker Inheritance* with a wealth of informational texts is an engaging introduction to research processes.

After curating their own Memorial Room, students can share their thinking with audiences beyond the school community. Teachers can register a class

YouTube account and help students develop an online tour of the classroom museum. Students can take turns filming their exhibits, narrating their curator descriptions, and uploading their pieces onto the class YouTube channel. Students can also encourage viewers to ask questions and give feedback in the comments section. This will give students the opportunity to have meaningful, ongoing dialogues about their work.

Sharing the Memorial Room with virtual audiences beyond the classroom reflects the ambition of NCTE/IRA Standard 8. Standard 8 reads: *Students use a variety of technological and informational resources to gather and synthesize information and to create and communicate knowledge.* Like Candice and Brandon, students can leverage their research to address audiences beyond their classrooms.

## CONCLUSION

In addition to its enthralling mystery, *The Parker Inheritance* asks timely questions about race, identity, and justice. By representing the ingenuity and genius of characters of Color, he inspires teachers and students to engage in similar critical excavations of history. Moving forward, teachers and students should keep an eye on Varian Johnson's important body of YA literature.

## REFERENCES

Bennett, B. (2020). *The vanishing half.* Riverhead Books.
Coates, T. (2018, May 7). *I'm not Black, I'm Kanye.* The Atlantic. https://www.the-atlantic.com
Johnson, V. (2018). *The parker inheritance.* Scholastic.
Raskin, E. (1978). *The westing game.* Penguin Random House.
Yang, R. (2019, October 11). *Cultural appropriation: What's an educator's role?* PBS Teachers Lounge. https://www.pbs.org/education/blog/

*Chapter 8*

# Renée Watson

## *Love Above All—Unpacking* Piecing Me Together

### Shanetia P. Clark

Renée Watson is an author, educator, poet, and activist who epitomizes #BlackGirlMagic. Her creative works and activism are anchored in love. Love of the word. Love of art. Love of self. Love of community. Love of family and friends. Love of the fullness of life. Love that celebrates and challenges. Love that critiques and pushes forward. Love moved her to lease and preserve the home of Harlem Renaissance poet Langston Hughes.

Watson founded the organization, the I, Too, Arts Collective, in order "to build upon Hughes' legacy by nurturing voices from underrepresented communities in the creative arts. We did this through commemorating, preserving, and activating the historic site with dynamic literary and cultural arts programming for established and youth writers alike" (I, Too, Arts Collective, nd.). The collective ceased operations in 2019, but the call to support new voices remains. Through the lens of love, Watson writes about Black characters who ask questions about their lives and about their world, and adolescent readers gravitate toward her work because she honors their lives.

Watson writes for all audiences. The picture book adaptation of Nicole Hannah-Jones's *The 1619 Project* is for young readers. In *The 1619 Project: Born on the Water* (2021), a picture book in verse, a Black elementary-aged girl's class was given an assignment: "Trace your roots. Draw a flag that represents your ancestral land" (p. 5). The girl leaves her paper blank because she does not know where her roots are. Saddened, she goes to her grandmother and explains her quandary. Her grandmother tells her that her roots did not start in 1619 when the first enslaved Africans were brought to Jamestown. Instead, she tells her granddaughter:

But before that dreadful voyage,
there was a time when they did not pray
for freedom.

There was a time when they did not sing
about overcoming.

Their story does not begin
with whips and chains.

They had a home, a place, a land,
a beginning.

Their story is our story.
Before they were
enslaved, they were
free.

She shares with her granddaughter the majesty, skills, and beauty of her ancestors.

Later, the grandmother does not shy away from the horrors of slavery: *"Ours is no immigration story"* (p. 11). These ancestors were stolen:

They did not get to pack bags stuffed
with cherished things, with the doll grandmama
had woven from tall grass,
with the baby blanket handed down
from generation to generation all the way back,
so far back that it carried the scent of the ancestors.

They could not hug their fathers and mothers,
daughters and sons,
hearts thumping in rhythm,
clinging to that final sweetness before the parting.
No promises, whispered from mouth to ear,
of seeing each other soon.

Not shying away from histories of Black people and doing so in a way that young children can understand is rooted in love. Love in being honest about the past is vitally important to Watson.

In her keynote speech at the Adolescent Literature Assembly of the National Council of Teachers of English (ALAN) workshop, Watson said when speaking about her book *Love is a Revolution*, "I was intentional about writing a story where Black teens are living their everyday lives, where Blackness is not a burden" (Watson, 2021, p. 14). Watson wants young people to not see their Blackness as a burden, even if the outside world tries to say so. Instead, it must be viewed as an asset, a beautiful gift.

She continues in her keynote speech, "Black teens live beyond racial injustice, and I believe we need more books that celebrate the fact that in a world that constantly tries to break them, they continue to show up, rise, try, smile. Doing all of that in the face of injustice, with the reminder that this world is not always welcoming—that is radical" (Watson, 2021, p. 14).

Renée Watson makes space for love that enables young people to critique their world. In her 2018 Newbery Honor Award and the Coretta Scott King Award-winning book *Piecing Me Together,* she tells the story of a young girl named Jade, who lives in Portland, Oregon. Watson, a Portland native, explains:

> As a child, it was rare to read stories about kids growing up in the Pacific Northwest, and the books that existed were about white characters. My teachers taught about the Great Migration to the North, but I did not learn how African Americans arrived in the Pacific Northwest. I learned about Lewis and Clark, but never about York. I was taught about segregation in Alabama, lynchings in Mississippi, but not about Portland's sundown laws. When I was in the fifth grade, skinheads beat an Ethiopian man to death with a baseball bat. Only one of my teachers talked about it in class.
>
> I wanted to talk about all of it. I needed a space to process what was happening in my neighborhood, in my world. (2018)

*Piecing Me Together* and Watson's other works are about finding a safe space to unpack and learn about the world for young readers. They can be used as a framework to provide the language to question, to be angry, to understand, and to wonder about the world.

The main character in *Piecing Me Together* explores and critiques the spaces and people around her. Jade lives in a majority Black neighborhood and takes the bus to her majority White private school. Her school counselor encourages her to participate in a mentorship program "Woman to Woman." After her counselor says that "[e]very young person could use a caring adult in her life," Jade pushes back on the assumption that her mother, uncle, and father don't care about her. Here, she criticizes the fact that her counselor revealed her racial bias.

The counselor quickly tries to clean up the microaggression: "We want to be as proactive as possible, and you know, well, statistics tell us that young people with your set of circumstances are, well, at risk for certain things, and we'd like to help you navigate through those circumstances" (2018, p. 18). Under the cloud of "good intentions," the counselor dismissed multiple aspects of the whole Jade and levied stereotypes of a broken home. She did not look beyond her circumstances to honor Jade's talents and intelligence.

Through Jade's experiences, readers can ask themselves, "How do I remain whole in a world that seems like it wants to break me? How do I make sure the story of my people and our experience is not erased?" (2018, para. 10). These questions are relevant today as young (and not so young) Black girls are under attack and are told to not take up their rightly deserved space or to even exist.

Jade is a young girl who begins to claim her space and to question spaces that try to diminish her right to do so. She exclaims:

> Sometimes I just want to be comfortable in this skin, this body. Want to cock my head back and laugh loud and free, all my teeth showing, and not be told I'm too rowdy, too ghetto. Sometimes I just want to go to school, wearing my hair big like cumulus clouds without getting any special attention, without having to explain why it looks different from the day before. Why it might look different tomorrow. Sometimes I just want to let my tongue speak the way it pleases, let it be untamed and not bound by rules. Want to talk without watchful ears listening to judge me. At school I turn on a switch, make sure nothing about me is too black. All day I am on. And that's why sometimes after school, I don't want to talk to Sam or go to her house, because her house is a reminder of how black I am. (p. 201)

Jade feels lonely as one of the only Black students at her school. She expresses frustration when she is passed over to study abroad, sighs at the audacity of the saleswoman who targets her in a store, and grumbles at a group of boys when they harassed her for ignoring them.

Jade uses art to express her emotions when words do not suffice. Her heart aches when a young Black girl had been brutalized by the police and not being able to talk through her sadness, fear, and anger with some people overwhelmed me. Through Jade, Watson challenges young readers to embrace the arts as a medium of expression. The use of collage is intentional. "What collage offers artists that cannot be found in flat work alone is the opportunity to add commentary through familiar imagery and objects. It adds to the dimension of the pieces and can further illustrate a point" (Gersh-Nesic, 2020).

## INSTRUCTIONAL ACTIVITIES

Watson's books enable adolescents to experience stories using metaphorical windows, mirrors, and sliding glass doors (Sims-Bishop, 1990). She explains:

> I write realistic fiction because I want young people and the adults in their lives to have a way to talk about what's happening, but have some space so you can

talk about the characters in the book, and not necessarily your own story yet, if you're not ready to have that conversation . . . And so I hope that my books provide space for young people to explore, and say, "Yeah, I feel seen." That's what I want young people to do—to talk to each other and to the adults in their lives.

The characters in her books engage with various mediums to express and to make sense of their feelings and surroundings.

The following "aesthetic education" inspired activities can be taught whole class, in small groups, or individually. Each has been inspired by *Piecing Me Together*. At their core, as philosopher and educator Maxine Greene explains, these experiences must extend encounters with and the creation of the arts and move toward the aesthetic. She notes that aesthetic education

> is an *intentional* undertaking designed to nurture, appreciate, reflective, cultural, *participatory engagements* with the arts by enabling learners to notice what there is to be noticed, and to lend works of arts their lives in such a way that they can achieve them as variously meaningful. When this happens, new connections are made in experience: new patterns are formed, new vistas are opened. Persons *see* differently, resonate different (Greene, 2001, p. 6). (emphasis added)

The following activities require that students are intentional and actively participate.

Jade is an artist. She creates collages in order to make "beauty out of everyday things—candy wrappers, pages of a newspaper, receipts, rip-outs from magazines. I cut and tear, arrange and rearrange, and glue them down, morphing them into something no one else thought they could be" (p. 10, Location 166). She is "rearranging reality, redefining, covering, disguising . . . [and] taking ugly and making beautiful" (p. 25, Location 330–322). This mission serves as the focus of her art.

## LOOKING BACK FOR INSPIRATION

Jade is introduced to African-American artists who pushed the narrative and made visible the lives of African-American people. When Jade shows Maxine, her mentor with Woman to Woman, her sketchbook with her brainstorms and some finished collages, Maxine exclaims, "Wow, Jade. You're like, a real artist. I mean--this isn't kid art. You are for real" (Watson, p. 41, location 498). Later during an outing to Powell's Bookstore, Maxine asks the clerk to show her artists who are collagists and African American.

The clerk immediately introduces Jade to the works of African-American collagists Romare Bearden and Mickalene Thomas (p. 77, Location 896). At Maxine's parents' home, artwork by Harlem Renaissance artist Jacob Lawrence hangs in the foyer. Also while at Maxine's friend Mia's gallery, Jade encounters the work of Kehinde Wiley.

For this first activity, investigate the work of the aforementioned artists— Romare Bearden, Mickalene Thomas, Jacob Lawrence, and Kehinde Wiley. While learning about these artists and their work, spend time actively engaged with their work. To help unpack, explore the "Capacities for Imaginative Learning" (Lincoln Center Institute, 2009). The first step for imaginative learning is to notice deeply, which is defined as "identify and articulate layers of detail in a work of art or other object of study through continuous interaction with it over time."

Noticing deeply, as well as other capacities—Embodying, Questioning, Identifying Patterns, Making Connections, Exhibiting Empathy, Living with Ambiguity, Creating Meaning, Taking Action, and Reflecting/Assessing— demand that the one who interacts with art must be engaged in conscious participation. In other words, invite students to actively ask questions about the art. Questions to guide the thinking include: *What do I notice? What do I wonder?* or *How does this work make me feel? What emotion or reaction do I think that the artist wanted to evoke?*

By slowing down and intentionally and deliberately viewing the work, students will be able to learn how the art was created; they will investigate the histories and contexts behind the works. For example, in *Piecing Me Together*, Mia's art gallery hangs the first series devoted to African-American women. The artist "used women from the streets of New York City as inspiration and based the poses off historical portraits by painters like Jacques-Louis David and other painters who almost exclusively painted white women" (Watson p. 227, Location 2407).

## EXPLORING AND OBSERVING FOR INSPIRATION

Another activity to do is to, like Jade, invite students and families/caregivers to explore their towns. Hidden stories may be discovered. For instance, while Jade rode the bus around Portland, she noticed a "larger-than-life" mural at the Oregon Historical Society building:

> The trompe l'oeil (pronounced "tromp la" or "tromp loi") mural, created by artist Richard Haas, depicts thirty-foot-high likenesses of Lewis and Clark Expedition members. Painted on the westward facing wall are: Meriwether

Lewis and William Clark; Sacagawea and her infant child, Baptiste; Clark's personal slave, York; and Lewis's Newfoundland, Seaman. (Randles, 2019)

This mural fascinates, haunts, and inspires Jade to take new risks and to ask questions and learn more about "invisible" stories of African Americans. Jade wants to know more about York. She wonders, "The whole time Lee Lee is talking, I am thinking about York and Sacagawea, wondering how they must have felt having a form of freedom but no real power" (Watson, 2017, p. 24).

Invite students to explore and observe their homes. Have them take pictures of things—buildings, people, or spaces—that are beautiful, unique, or want to know more about. Have them engage in research projects to learn of the stories behind the beauty.

## LOOKING INWARD AND SPEAKING OUTWARD FOR INSPIRATION

Maxine Greene wrote in her groundbreaking article "Art and Imagination: Reclaiming the Sense of Possibility," "[participatory] involvement with the many forms of art does enable us, at the very least, to *see* more in our experience, to *hear* more on normally unheard frequencies, to *become conscious* of what daily, routines, habits, and conventions have obscured" (Greene, 1995, p. 379). Each requires that young people become completely and wholly invested in their creation and experiences.

Maxine Greene reminds us that

> [mere] exposure to a work of art is not sufficient to occasion an aesthetic experience. There must be conscious participation in a work, a going out of energy, an ability to notice what is there to be noticed in the play, the poem, the quartet. "Knowing about," even in the most formal academic manner, is entirely different from creating an unreal world imaginatively and entering it perceptually, affectively, and cognitively.

The final instructional idea amplifies this assertion.

Invite young people to create a self-portrait using the medium that Jade employs—collage. Students may use a portrait that depicts their physical likeness, but they may also collage to embody their inner feelings. In other words, they are creating a "self-portrait" of their inner spirit. Upon finishing their masterpiece, have students title with work and write and share poems or paragraphs inspired by the work. Both the written piece and the artwork will be shared as a unit. Also, have students list the materials used in the creation of the artwork.

## CONCLUSION

Renée Watson is a treasure. Anchored in the spirit and movement of love, she has provided a beautiful bounty of books that speak to the experiences and dreams of young Black people. Her books hold the space for Black adolescents. This space makes room for them to question, to create, to critique, to advocate, and to love. Her books, in particular *Piecing Me Together*, honor the lives of young people. She centers on Black characters, experiences, and audiences, and that makes Renée Watson and her extensive bibliography a safe haven.

## OTHER WORKS BY RENEE WATSON

*This Side of Home* (2015)
*Love is a Revolution* (2021)
*Black Enough: Stories of Being Young and Black in America* (2019, edited by Ibi Zoboi)
*Some Places More than Others* (2019)
*What Momma Left Me* (2019)
*Ways to Make Sunshine: A Ryan Hart Story* (2020)
*The Talk: Conversations about Race, Love & Truth* (2020, edited by Cheryl and Wade Hudson)
*The 1619 Project: Born on the Water* (2021, coauthored with Nicole Hannah-Jones)

## REFERENCES

Bishop, R. S. (1990). Mirrors, windows, and sliding glass doors. *Perspectives: Choosing and Using Books for the Classroom*, 6(3), ix–xi.

Gersh-Nesic, B. (2020, August 28). How is collage used in art? Retrieved from https://www.thoughtco.com/art-history-definition-collage-183196

Greene, M. (1995). Art and imagination: Reclaiming the sense of possibility. *The Phi Delta Kappan, 76*(5), 378–382. Retrieved January 1, 2021, from http://www.jstor.org/stable/20405345.

Randles, R. (2019). "Is it flat? Illusion, reality, and the Haas mural." Retrieved from https://www.ohs.org/blog/is-it-flat.cfm.

Watson, R. (2017). *Piecing me together* [eBook edition]. Bloomsbury.

Watson, R. (2021). Keynote at the ALAN Workshop. *The ALAN Review*.

## Chapter 9

# Tiffany D. Jackson

## *Shining a Light on Missing Black Girls through Creative Narratives in* Monday's Not Coming

### Steven T. Bickmore and Gretchen Rumohr

Few authors arrive on the landscape of young adult (YA) literature with a bigger splash within a four-year period than Tiffany D. Jackson. Her first book, *Allegedly*, arrived quietly in 2017 and many scholars missed its debut. Fortunately, it was nominated for an NAACP Image Award for Outstanding Literary Work. The secret of her talent was over. A year later, advanced readers' copies of *Monday's Not Coming* (2018) arrived. By 2019, *Let Me Hear a Rhyme* was published, and Jackson was a featured speaker at the 2019 ALAN Workshop. Jackson hasn't slowed down, publishing *Grown* in 2020 and three more books in 2021.

### JACKSON'S CRITICAL RECEPTION

Tiffany Jackson's work in film and television—especially in suspense and horror genres—has served her well. Jackson's first two novels can be classified as complex suspense novels with questionable narrators and plot narratives that are complicated but well worth the reader's attention. Like the renowned Joyce Carol Oates, Jackson takes her cues from real-life, newsworthy events and topics, molding them into powerful narratives. Her next two novels, *Let Me Hear a Rhyme* (2019) and *Grown* (2020), are connected to the music industry.

Jackson's books have received remarkable critical acclaim and multiple starred reviews. Yet the most important recognition to date is her reception of the John Steptoe Award for New Talent. This is an award under the umbrella of the American Library Association and awarded by the Coretta Scott King Book Awards Committee with specific requirements. An author can only receive the award once, must not have more than three published works, and can not have been a winner of one of the Coretta Scott King awards in the current year. Past winners include Sharon G. Flake, Sharon Draper, Jason Reynolds, and Kekla Magoon.

Winning such an award catapults an author into a field of awareness that assures that the next several works will receive the attention of scholars, librarians, and teachers at various levels of education. It also makes it more likely that the publication house will more actively promote the author's work at conferences, conventions, and through book tours. Clearly, Ms. Jackson's star and productivity are on the rise.

In 2021, Jackson published the horror novel *White Smoke* (2021) with a starred review from Kirkus. This book builds on the horror genre that Jackson has used in the film industry. She also teamed up with a daughter of Malcom X, Ilyasah Shabazz, for *The Awakening of Malcolm* (2021), which creatively images Malcolm's self-education while in prison and his transition from Malcolm Little to Malcolm X.

She is also included in an anthology, *Blackout* (2021), with five other emerging black female authors—Dhonielle Clayton, Nic Stone, Angie Thomas, Ashley Wookfolk, and Nicola Yoon. The focus of this chapter, the novel *Monday's Not Coming*, has also received notable acclaim, including starred reviews from *School Library Journal* and *Bulletin of the Center for Children's Books*. Few authors achieve this number of publications in a five-year period, and even fewer do so with such a high level of literary quality. From her first book's recognition at the NAACP image awards to the second receiving the Steptoe Award, who knows what awaits for Jackson?

## A CRITICAL DISCUSSION OF *MONDAY'S NOT COMING*

*Monday's Not Coming* exemplifies Jackson's trademark talents: horrifying plotlines with believable (but ultimately unreliable) narrators. While the book is more than 450 pages, it is a quick and riveting read. The novel features Claudia, whose best friend, Monday Charles, has gone missing when Claudia needs her help to face bullies and a learning disability. From various details shared, it is apparent that Monday lives in project housing with few resources as well as an abusive mother. Claudia's teachers, parents, and friends cannot give her a straight answer; they can't remember when they last saw Monday, or where she may have gone.

Ultimately, it is revealed that Monday (along with her younger brother) has been murdered and stashed in a chest freezer. With that revelation, all hell breaks loose: Due to this traumatic information, Claudia's perception of the events (and their sequence) becomes fuzzy; even the timeline of Claudia's own life is compromised, leaving the reader disoriented yet still engaged.

Regardless of *how* and *when* things happen in this book, truths remain: Monday is a Black girl who lived in the projects, and her very home was threatened with gentrification. Monday is a Black girl who was loved like a sister by Claudia. Monday is a Black girl who was brutally murdered and then hidden in a buzzing freezer, and no one seemed to ask any questions about where she had gone. For many reasons, Monday was forgotten.

The book is rich with opportunities for critical lenses, though considering Tyson's *Critical Theory Today: A User-Friendly Guide* (2015) in the context of *Monday's Not Coming*, an African-American critical lens brings meaningful discovery. Readers can focus on issues such as the "difficulties of economic survival" as seen by multiple characters in the text, especially Monday's father and his employment struggles as they relate to his child support payments; "institutionalized racism" and "oppression of racism, classism, and sexism" as applied to the Monday's project housing (Tyson, 2015, p. 385).

Readers can also consider issues of Black invisibility in a world that favors white voices as everyone seems to have forgotten about Monday and doesn't seem to take Claudia's concerns about Monday's disappearance seriously (Tyson, 2015, p. 387) as well as the idea of the "suspended woman" who has no agency over a life of abuse (p. 390). Psychoanalytic criticism (especially with discussions of the fear of death, the existence of death drives, and how trauma influences memory loss) and Marxism (considering how economic forces contribute to Monday's death and others' lack of awareness about it) can also be utilized (pp. 21–14).

## BEFORE-READING ACTIVITIES

Given that *Monday's Not Coming* is a frank depiction of the blight of public housing and the manner in which the disappearance of black girls is marginalized at best, and, more accurately, ignored completely by media reporting, it's important to note that adolescents often know more than adults give them credit for about the reality of the world around them. They often know who is hungry, who is lonely, who is a latchkey child, whose parents are going through a divorce, who is skipping school, who is using illegal substances, and who is probably missing.

Even with this information, most adolescents who live in blighted neighborhoods, public housing, and other marginalized communities manage their daily lives fairly successfully. Indeed, most outside observers might be persuaded that their lives are normal. Yet, in reality, they are often quietly doing the best they can. At the same time, students probably have very little understanding of the laws, policies, and community practices that influence housing, social safety nets, policing, and media coverage—especially in the context of institutionalized racism.

Given the frank and difficult topic of this book, it might be best approached as a selection for literature circle selection rather than as a book for full class discussion. How, then, can a teacher construct a set of activities that engage students in building a knowledge base around these topics? How can this knowledge base help to answer an essential question (Wilhelm, 2020): Why does society forget about certain people, and what can be done about it? The following series of activities help students explore these important topics as well as the essential question through independent exploration, group work, and whole-class engagement.

The first step to exploring the text—which will connect to the after-reading activity—is to introduce students to the Steptoe Award. After providing them with the link to the web page. Students are asked to explore at least five YA authors. Depending on how familiar the students are with exploring concepts on the web, the teacher can provide recommendations. For example, students can visit authors' webpages, sources that review books, like Kirkus, the New York Times Book Review, or the Guardian, and blogs like Dr. Bickmore's YA Wednesday or the Nerdy Book Club (see textbox 9.1 for a list of all referenced websites.)

## TEXTBOX 9.1

### URLs Referenced in the Chapter

Kirkus Book Reviews: https://www.kirkusreviews.com/
New York Times Book Review: https://www.nytimes.com/section/books/review
The Guardian Books: https://www.theguardian.com/books
Dr. Bickmore's YA Wednesday: http://www.yawednesday.com/
Nerdy Book Club: https://nerdybookclub.wordpress.com/
John Steptoe New Talent Award: https://www.ala.org/rt/emiert/cskbookawards/johnsteptoe
Read Write Think: https://www.readwritethink.org/

With this activity, students track their exploration and demonstrate that they have visited at least three sources per author. Students should note in their classroom journals which authors they investigated, what information the sources shared, and how these authors engage with various social issues. Students will set aside this information until after they are done reading the book.

## Individual

Students need more practice researching and documenting ideas from primary and secondary sources, and there are ways that such research and documentation can help them answer the essential question in the context of the book. In this independent research project, a brief, self-guided research project, the teacher creates a list of topics related to the plot and the setting of *Monday's Not Coming* (see textbox 9.2). Topics can include "trauma and memory loss," "gone and forgotten Black girls," "redlining/segregated housing," "Black unemployment," and "racial and ethnic disparity in prisons."

---

**TEXTBOX 9.2**

Research topics related to *Monday's Not Coming*

1. Missing girls in the United States—especially Black girls
2. The treatment of young women in various other countries India— child labor, Thailand
3. The history of public housing in the United States especially in large Urban Centers. How big are they in terms of capacity?
4. Who are the people maintaining public housing and how do they do it?
5. How many are now deserted or torn down?
6. Where were they located in the first place and for what reasons? What is the role of redlining?
7. What are the educational systems like near public housing projects?
8. What are the employment rates of people in public housing vs. rates in other parts of the city? How do employment rates in all communities vary by race and gender?
9. What are the causes of childhood trauma and how frequently is memory loss part of this trauma?
10. What are the rates of racial and ethnic disparity in prisons and jails? How does this vary from community to community, state to state, and within the federal system?

---

To expedite finding quality research, the teacher could collect links to relevant articles, creating an informal "WebQuest" for students as they research. Time given can vary depending on how many sources the teacher desires for students to read. In the spirit of Claudia's letters to Monday, students are partnered with a classmate, asked to acknowledge the essential question, and write a letter that relates the essential question to what they learned on their topic.

A student researching "gone and forgotten Black girls" could talk about how the media's role and how necessary information does not reach the public, contributing to the "forgetting."

The teacher can decide to allow students to choose a topic if this will be the only pre-reading activity before reading the text. However, if conducting all activities, the teacher will assign students a topic in order to facilitate the small group work.

## Small Group

### *Jigsaw Activity*

A jigsaw activity helps students work together in more than one group and holds each student accountable for the work required. Students do work in one group that is different from the other groups in the class, and must participate and learn the material as an "expert" so that when groups are reformed in the class—with a single member from each group—they relay, in turn, the information from their group to the others.

This activity can be done at a level of basic literary analysis or with a focus on the essential question as well as thematic issues in the book. Reading aloud picture books such as *Milo's Museum* (Elliott & Wong, 2016) or *The Fair Housing Five and the Haunted House* (Madhi-Neville, 2010) can initiate discussions about systemic racism as well as provide a backdrop for literary terms suggested below.

A class of twenty students can first focus on studying a description of literary elements, with five groups of four students. Each group can be assigned a letter and each student assigned a number from 1 to 4. Then each group can be assigned a different topic: Group A, *characterization*; Group B, *setting*; Group C, *symbols*; Group D, *(un)reliable narrator*; and Group E, *important plot elements* (exposition, rising action, climax, falling action, resolution).

Students should be able to define and then provide examples of their topic in the context of the picture books referenced above. Depending on their knowledge and work habits, students can be provided with an adequate amount of time—20–30 minutes—to research, discuss, and prepare talking points with evidence from the text and secondary sources. This activity can either (1) serve to introduce students to the description and recognition of literary elements if the concepts are new or (2) serve to reinforce what students have already learned about literary elements in a previous course as they prepare to study *Monday's Not Coming*.

After groups are divided by letter as specified above, they are divided by number. Now, all of the ones form a group, the twos as well, and so on. Since the groups are reformed there are five members and each should take 5 minutes to present the information they have mastered with their new group. It is not necessary that the two groups meet on the same day. In fact, giving members the opportunity to review their notes and prepare their presentations might be beneficial for many students. The activity allows students to work together knowing that each member will be responsible to master the information and share it with others to the degree that they can master it as well.

For the work with *Monday's Not Coming*, a teacher might do the jigsaw activity twice: once exploring literary elements, and a second time with topics students studied in the self-guided research project (refer again to textbox 9.2). The second option works well as teachers prepare five different research topics with four students assigned to each, thus creating the core "first" lettered groups. Students come to the activity prepared to share with others who have studied the same topic. As a result, the expected level of production can be higher than the activity on literary elements that can be done without advance preparation.

*Whole Class*

Taking their jigsaw activity further, in the small groups they create a poster or an infographic with key information about the topic they explored. These infographics should in some way attempt to answer the essential question: Why does society forget about certain people, and what can be done about it? For the whole-group activity, each group will present the concept and then display the infographic. The teacher can also ask each group to prepare a set of discussion questions. Ideally, the students can conduct the discussion while the teacher watches and monitors engagement.

## During-Reading Activities

*Individual*

Students can choose two or three topics from their before-reading activities and then look for relevant passages that activate and enrich this prior knowledge. Students catalog this information in a class journal, helping them to build a collection of passages that can be used to construct a presentation or conduct a conversation on how the topic is evident in the book. In addition, these pages can be used to establish citational authority for an analytical essay that might be used as a summative assessment.

## Small Group

In a tableau activity (Wilhelm, 2002), the teacher assigns scenes from the book that speak to the essential question. For example, scenes that help students consider "Why does society forget about certain people, and what can be done about it?" include Claudia telling her mother about how Monday didn't show up for the first day of school; Claudia asking her teacher about Monday; Claudia's various recollections of Monday's difficult home situation; Claudia's "undercover" visit to Monday's home; Claudia and Michael's visit to Monday's father; Claudia asking the school nurse about Monday; and Claudia's final breakdown at school.

Other relevant passages can be assigned provided that they relate to answering the essential question. The teacher divides students into groups and assigns them a few relevant passages. Students are told to read through the passage and then "block" that scene as a freeze-frame that encapsulates the most important part of that scene. Students will "rehearse" these freeze-frame tableaus and then the teacher will facilitate a whole-class sharing, having students perform these tableaus in the order of plot events so that there is a snapshot retelling of the story.

Upon watching, students can be asked: Why did you choose this particular pose? What, in your opinion, is the most important part of this scene? What did you discover about the book/characters/plot/issue as a result of this scene? At the end of the tableau activity, questions can be broadened to the essential question: What did we learn about how society forgets from "retelling" these plot events?

## Whole Class

Throughout Jackson's book, there are opportunities to stop and ask students what issues they are noticing or struggling with (related to themselves, or society as a whole); their class journal can document these struggles. Students can identify these issues and then create a KWL chart: What do they know about this issue already (K); what do they want to know (W), and what they've learned (L).

With this KWL, students can revisit their self-guided research projects, this time focusing on broader questions: missing indigenous populations; gerrymandering and its effect on governmental representation; the affordable housing crisis; the Flint water issue; the compromised health of Black women. Students can be encouraged to examine social media influencer activists and note important hashtags; they can research these hashtags for additional information.

Finally, students can determine if there are local implications for the above issues and whether such issues are represented in *Monday's Not Coming*. Students can be paired with their original letter-writing partners to verbally share their KWL charts and then share their favorite discoveries verbally in a whole-group discussion.

## Post-Reading Activities

### *Individual*

The John Steptoe New Talent Award is one of the most prestigious awards that a new author can receive. Sponsored by the American Library Association, it began in 1995 with an award to Sharon Draper. With few exceptions, it has been given every year. Several winners were included in volume two of this series *Expanding the Foundation* (2022) and others are in this current volume. Without exception, the authors and books that were recognized for the award are all worth reading. Unfortunately, many teachers don't know them and even fewer students have read them.

Much of the impetus of all three volumes in this series is to bring more awareness to these African-American authors. Their contributions have been both foundational and inspirational. As students begin a post-reading activity focused on an author who has one the Steptoe New Talent Award or another Coretta Scott King Award, the teacher might provide an overview of the awards the authors treated in this series. Refer to textbox 9.3 for a synopsis of their awards. (We have only included five major awards here, but there are many more that a teacher might reference.)

The class has now read and studied *Monday's Not Coming* and given their before, during- and after-reading activities, they have been primed to discover other noted winners of the Steptoe Award. The teacher can tell students that now that they have finished *Monday's Not Coming*, the teacher informs the students that their individual post-reading assignment will be reading and studying a book by another winner of the Steptoe Award.

Part of the assignment will be to compare the literary quality of their "winning" novel against Jackson's novel. While studying their choice, they should consider how the author presents themes, plot, symbols, character development, and other aspects of literature typically discussed in ELA class. They should also be ready to comment on how their chosen author engages in answering the essential question.

## TEXTBOX 9.3

### Notable literary awards and awardees

*Awards: King Award (KA) Steptoe Award (SA) Newbery Winner (N) Newbery Honor (H) National Book Award (NB)*

**Book 1 On the Shoulders of Giants: Celebrating African American Authors of Young Adult Literature**

| | |
|---|---|
| Virginia Hamilton | *KA* 1983, 1986, 1996; *H* 1972, 1983, 1989; *N* 1975 |
| Walter Dean Myers | *KA* 1980, 1985, 1989, 1992, 1997; *NB* 2005, 2010 |
| Julius Lester | *KA* 2006; *H* 1969 |
| Mildred Taylor | *KA* 1982, 1988, 1991, 2002; *N* 1977 |

**Book 2 Expanding the Foundation: African American Authors of Young Adult Literature, 1980–2000**

| | |
|---|---|
| Jacqueline Woodson | *KA* 2001, 2015, 2021; *H* 2006, 2008, 2009; *NB* 2002, 2003, 2014 |
| Angela Johnson | *KA* 1999, 2004 |
| Nikki Grimes | *KA* 2003 |
| Sharon Draper | *KA* 1998, 2007; *SA* 1995 |
| Christopher Paul Curtis | *KA* 2000, 2008; *H* 1996, 2008; *N* 2000 |
| Sharon G. Flake | *SA* 1999 |
| Rita Williams-Garcia | *KA* 2011, 2014, 2016; *H* 2011; *NB* 2009, 2010, 2017 |

**Book 3 A Period of Growth in African American Young Adult Literature: More Mirrors, Windows, and Sliding Doors**

| | |
|---|---|
| Shelia P. Moses | *NB* 2004 |
| Kwame Alexander | *N* 2015; *H* 2020 |
| Kekla Magoon | *SA* 2010; *NB* 2021 |
| Jason Reynolds | *SA* 2015; *H* 2018; *NB* 2016, 2019 |
| Renée Watson | *KA* 2018; *H* 2018 |
| Tiffany D. Jackson | *SA* 2019 |

The best reading is self-engaged reading. Nevertheless, while students are reading they need to keep in mind that they will be sharing their observations of their selection with others. Students can track how literary elements are evident in the book. Placing different colored post-it notes for each device or creating a chart that tracks page numbers can be a helpful way for students to track important information without distracting from their reading. In addition, students should consider stopping after reading each chapter and think about what might be important points to remember for their future presentations.

## Small Group

The poster-presentation activity reminds both teachers and students that ELA classes include more than reading and writing. It is important to practice the speaking and listening skills that come from planning a presentation and then presenting it formally or informally with others. For this activity, the teacher organizes the class into small groups with students who have read the same Steptoe award-winning author.

Once the students have finished reading the book, the students meet together to plan a poster that presents the author. They might include the awards, quotes from reviews, a photo of the author, cover art, biographical information, and a variety of other information that might serve to introduce the author to others. Posters can be designed in the traditional ways by supplying students with poster board and art supplies. Nevertheless, teachers should remind students that we are now firmly in a digital age. Students will be required to present their ideas in sophisticated ways paying attention to design and message.

A good starting point for poster instruction is to investigate the resources on NCTE's Read Write Think feature. One resource, a series of lessons, is Traci Gardner's Designing effective poster presentations. A teacher can familiarize herself with these concepts and provide mini-lessons for the students throughout the unit so that they are prepared as they finish their books and begin group work. Of course, both teachers and students can find a number of other sources online by conducting an internet search on How to Create a Poster. The results will suggest a number of apps that provide free or relatively cheap access to wonderful tools.

Once the small groups have held several sessions, perhaps one to gather the information, another to organize a mocked-up design on a sheet of paper, and another to create the poster, the teacher is ready to organize a mode of presentation. Teachers organize a gallery walk that allows five of the twenty students to present during each of four sessions. Each session is only 8–10 minutes. The other fifteen students select one poster session and settle in to listen to the presentation. Each student will then have the opportunity to present once and also listen to three other presentations.

Such an activity allows students to both present and listen. Too often students are not given the opportunity to report on what they have heard during a presentation. This can be accomplished in a number of ways. The most direct way is to ask the student to report on which book they might like to read next and what information in the presentation persuaded them to select this book. Teachers might employ more rigorous requirements that might require them to rank presentations based on a rubric or to ask them to complete the two parts of a KWL chart on each author that will be presented before the gallery walk and then complete it after.

## Whole Class

Students can share their "award" novel with a four-minute presentation in the style of Penny Kittle's (2013) *Book Love*. The presentation should include a brief introduction to the author, a brief summary of why the book is award-worthy, a reading of a short passage that will "hook" other readers, and (if the book is available), an opportunity to pass the book around so that classmates can read further or examine the cover.

Through these book talks, students have opportunities to ask themselves some important questions: how do authors answer "big questions"? What gives a book literary merit? How are authors recognized for their work? (This question, of course, is an opportunity to also examine how many worthy authors are *not* recognized and how systemic racism persists in the publishing industry.)

Finally, students should revisit their letter-writing activity—and their essential question—one last time before finishing the unit. As they write to their classmates, they can be asked: Why does society forget about certain people, and what can be done about it? What did Tiffany Jackson do about it? What did my "award" author do about it? What can *I* do about it? This time, their classmates can be directed to write back, lauding their discoveries and choices and suggesting further actions.

## BEYOND THE BOOK, A "FIRST PAGES" ACTIVITY

Students can consider additional titles with a "First Pages" activity. The teacher can gather "first pages" from five National Book Award finalists that address systemic racism. The teacher gives 3 minutes for students to read each "first" page and then asks: how is systemic racism present on that first page (if it isn't; discuss how authors share thematic information)? What is the tone? Who is represented on the first page? What do we know about the characters/plot so far? What seem to be the main conflicts so far? From what you've read on the first page, why do you want to keep reading? What do you feel is award-worthy so far?

Giving students the opportunity to do think-pair-shares, and then whole-group sharing allows for ample discussion and discovery about reading closely and inferring context. Varying this activity to include the teacher distributing actual National Book Award finalist (or other award category) books to each student can also initiate a brief book talk share-out, allowing students to gather book recommendations from their fellow classmates.

## AUTHOR'S WORKS

Jackson, T. D. (2017). *Allegedly: a novel* (1st ed.). New York: Katherine Tegen Books, an imprint of HarperCollins Publishers.

Jackson, T. D. (2018). *Monday's not coming: a novel* (1st ed.). New York: Katherine Tegen Books, an imprint of HarperCollins Publishers.

Jackson, T. D. (2020). *Grown: a novel* (1st ed.). New York: Katherine Tegen Books, an imprint of HarperCollins Publishers.

Jackson, T. D. (2021). *White smoke* (1st ed.) New York: Katherine Tegen Books, an imprint of HarperCollins Publishers.

Jackson, T. D., & Brown, R. (2021). *Santa in the city.* New York: Dial Books for Young Readers.

Jackson, T. D., & Sharif, M. (2019). *Let me hear a rhyme* (1st ed.). New York: Katherine Tegen Books, an imprint of HarperCollins Publishers.

Jackson, T. D., Stone, N., Woodfolk, A., Clayton, D., Thomas, A., & Yoon, N. (2021). *Blackout* (1st ed.). New York: Quill Tree Books, an imprint of HarperCollins Publishers.

## REFERENCES

Elliott, Z., & Wong, P. (2016). *Milo's museum.* Rosetta Press.

Kittle, P. (2013). *Book love: Developing depth, stamina, and passion in adolescent readers.* Heinemann.

Mahdi-Neville, S. (2010). *The fair housing five & the haunted house.* Greater New Orleans Fair Housing Action Center.

Tyson, L. (2015). *Critical theory today: A user-friendly guide.* Routledge.

Wilhelm, J. D. (2002). *Action strategies for deepening comprehension.* New York: Scholastic Inc.

Wilhelm, J. D., Bear, R., & Fachler, A. (2020). *Planning powerful instruction: 7 must-make moves to transform how we teach—and how students learn.* Corwin.

*Chapter 10*

# Nnedi Okorafor

## *The Future Begins with an Alternative Origin Story*

### Oluwaseun Animashaun

In a brief interlude of Okorafor's *Who Fears Death*, our one-time narrator, Sola, translates the Nsibidi peacock symbol drawn by our imprisoned protagonist, Onyensonwu. The sign means "one is going to take action" (Okorafor, 2010, p. 383). Sola continues with the explanation: "Is it not understandable that she'd want to live in the very world she helped remake? That indeed is a more logical destiny" (ibid). It is impossible to reflect on the significance and potency of this revelation without discussing how Okorafor's origins and actions have produced a seismic shift in literary community.

While the above excerpt ostensibly concerns Okorafor's boundary-destroying protagonist, it also gorgeously speaks to Okorafor's space-making and world-building that has offered a place for African readers and authors who have been marginalized in the Western science fiction community. In this chapter, I provide a brief exploration of Okorafor's origins and oeuvre as a foundation to critically engage with her artistic offerings.

Raised in "very racist, very white" (D'arcy, 2018) Chicago suburb of South Holland, Illinois, Nnedi Okorafor was abundantly clear on her status as an outsider. Born to Nigerian parents, who immigrated due to the Nigerian Civil War, she was "seen as 'too black' to hang out with her white neighbors, but on visits to Nigeria, she was viewed by cousins there as being 'too American'" (ibid).

It is not the race alone that has crafted Okorafor's social position as other. In a *Locus Magazine* interview, she explains that along with her Nigerian-American background, her former paralysis and invisible disability have also been reasons for her otherness, but she was "always been one to embrace those things, as opposed to lamenting the difficulties" (*Locus Magazine*, 2021).

Okorafor was a child who lived in the gray areas within boundaries. She moved in and through those permeable spaces and built worlds that could fit the whole of her thoughts, feelings, actions, histories—her existence. While being seen as "other" or outsider can be a source of harm or trauma or a cause to erase the differences, Okorafor explains that "there was never a time where [she] felt like [she] had to try to be someone else to fit in" (D'arcy, 2018).

It is the practice of observing and honoring her otherness as well as imagining worlds where whole selves can move freely that Okorafor's relationship with the science fiction genre emerges. Okorafor has wielded the science fiction genre to spark the imaginations of folx who are otherwise missing that expression in their daily lives (ibid). In the introduction to graphic novel adaptation of *Kindred*, she writes of an encounter with Octavia Butler's *Wild Seed*—"As I strolled through the aisles, something extraordinary caught my eye, something I'd only ever seen once before in the science fiction and fantasy section of a bookstore: a cover featuring a dark-skinned black woman" (Duffy et al., 2017, p. iv).

Years later Okorafor would be penning adaptation for Butler's works for graphic novels and television. More importantly, *Wild Seed* affirmed Okorafor's belief that there was a space for Black and African folx in the genre of science fiction as she was emerging as a science fiction writer in her own right. It had "'proved that what [Okorafor] was writing was okay, that people like [her] could be a part of this canon. This was a *very* big deal'" (ibid). In reaching for worlds that center the lives, histories, and cultures on the African continent, Okorafor coined, popularized as a subgenre of science/ speculative fiction—*Africanfuturism.*

According to her blog,

Africanfuturism is specifically and more directly rooted in African culture, history, mythology and point-of-view as it then branches into the Black Diaspora, and it does not privilege or center the West. Africanfuturism is concerned with visions of the future, is interested in technology, leaves the earth, skews optimistic, is centered on and predominantly written by people of African descent (black people) and it is rooted first and foremost in Africa. It's less concerned with "what could have been" and more concerned with "what is and can/will be." It acknowledges, grapples with and carries "what has been." (Okorafor, 2019)

Okorafor's visioning of Africanfuturism centers on three critical ideas.

First, Africanfuturism is about African peoples—their lived experiences, spiritualities and stories in the past, present, and future. Second, Africanfuturism forward a technologically advanced Africa that has a stake in national, global, and universal affairs. Third and lastly, the genre advances the traditions, present, and futurities simultaneously of Africa, without the distraction of rewriting history. While Okorafor coined this term, she acknowledges that "African science fiction's blood runs deep and it's old, and it's ready to come forth, and when it does, imagine the new technologies, ideas and sociopolitical changes it'll inspire" (Okorafor, 2017).

Okorafor has been exceedingly prolific. She has written *Who Fears Death*, the Binti novella trilogy, *The Book of Phoenix*, the Akata books, and *Lagoon*, to name a few. When she is not writing novels, she is developing television series: *Who Fears Death* and Butler's *Wild Seed*. Amid novel publications and television screenplays, she has written graphic novels *LaGuardia* and *Black Panther: Long Live the King*, *Wakanda Forever*, and *Shuri* the series. Okorafor's extensive catalog has not gone unwitnessed as she has been the recipient of myriad awards including the Hugo, Nebula, Locus, Caine, World Fantasy, and Lodestar awards. Like the Nsibidi peacock symbol suggest, she has taken action to create worlds worthy of the lives they hold.

## HARMONIZING WITH BINTI: CRITICAL ENGAGEMENT WITH THE NOVELLA

*Binti* is an Africanfuturist space opera that follows our eponymous heroine as she has decided to leave her family home and country of Namibia— against her family's wishes and traditions—to pursue her dreams of attending a prominent university in outer space. Along the way, her peers are massacred, and she alone is left alive, a captive of the Meduse, an alien race. On borrowed time, Binti attempts to survive this horrific experience as the spaceship continues to make its way to the university with an enemy force onboard.

Okorafor explains in her TED Talk that she wrote this story "because of blood that runs deep, family, cultural conflict and the need to see an African girl leave the planet on her own terms. My science fiction had different ancestors, African ones" (Okorafor, 2017). With a new starting point—an African starting point—Okorafor sets readers on a reality governed by an alternative set of rules.

Namibia conjured in *Binti* counters stereotypes of Africa as desert wasteland, populated with impoverished and technologically inferior peoples. It does not partake in the long tradition of Western writing that solely situates Africans as people perpetually in need of aid. Binti regales readers with a description of her family home, the Root as "the oldest house in my village, maybe the oldest in the city. It was made of stone and concrete . . . and it

was patched with solar planes and covered with bioluminescent plants"
(Okorafor, p. 12–13).

This gorgeous union of African architecture, nature, as well as contemporary technology presents tradition and modernity as compatible projects. This
futuristic Namibian city is a site of intellectual prowess and self-sustainability
that simultaneously honors and sustains the land, its nonhuman and human
inhabitants. *Binti* demolishes the deficit lens through which Western media
has portrayed Africa and her peoples.

## Binti's Identity and Culture

Binti adheres to the design Okorafor usually employs for her protagonists:
a young woman who is a part of and apart from her community, is "caught
between cultures and worlds, navigating remarkable circumstances" (D'arcy,
2018). Despite her differences, Binti embraces her whole self as she "goes
out as she is, looking the way she looks, carrying her cultures, being who she
is" (Okorafor, 2017). Similar to their author, she fashions a space for herself
in a universe questioning her existence. Binti gifts readers an opportunity to
understand how race, gender, and cultural expectations can collide to produce
both oppressive conditions and fantastic possibilities.

Outside of her homeland, Binti's cultural habits are "othered" and consequently, a site of ridicule. Her debut among the Khoush—a White non-
Himba people—is steeped in horrors at every turn. A Khoush stranger tugs
at Binti's body without consent to learn of the *otjize* (reddish clay) that
styles her hair and embellishes her skin. Another Khoush stranger admon-
ishes the Himba as "dirt bathers" and a "filthy people" (Okorafor, 2015,
p. 15). The leering and jeering metamorphose into requests to minimize her
otherness.

On the spaceship, Binti is the recipient of sharp requests—"Wear your
*otjize* . . . But not so much that you stain up this ship" (Okorafor, 2015, p. 21).
While she is permitted to carry her culture, it is to be in tolerable amounts—
less obscene to those who do not understand. Yet, even with a constant
stream of degrading experiences, Binti remembers, honors, and protects her
difference.

Instead of relegating Binti's difference to a source of pain, Okorafor pro-
motes it as an entry point for Binti to approach and generate a shared foundation with her Meduse captors. Okwu, the Meduse who speaks with Binti,
describes their understanding of humans in this world—"The Khoush are the
color of the flesh of the fish you ate and they have no okuoko. You are red
brown like the fish's outer skin and you have okuoko like Meduse, though
small" (Okorafor, 2015, p. 54). Binti's race shares a similar spiritual or ener-
getic flow that the Meduse have and cultivate. It is this difference, among

others, that Binti possesses—that propels her into the unique position to save herself and save the world.

## Questions about the Pursuit of Knowledge

Okorafor interrogates the pursuits of knowledge. Throughout the novella, various characters are challenged, antagonized, strengthened, victimized by the consequences of others' thirst for knowledge.

The Himba tribe is described as "obsessed with innovation technology . . . [but] don't like to leave Earth. [They] prefer to explore the universe by traveling inward, as opposed to outward" (Okorafor, 2015, p. 21). This understanding of exploration and knowledge comes in direct opposition to Binti's desire to leave and learn elsewhere. Consequently, this juxtaposition births internal turmoil for Binti. Which knowledge is worth pursuing? Where can knowledge be located? Is it worth possibly shaming her family and severing ties to her land, ancestral and communal traditions?

While Binti chooses to seek a life beyond her immediate locale, she does bear witness to the harm these outward reaches for knowledge can become for others. Okorafor reveals the reason for the Meduse's attack: restitution. After their chief was attacked and mutilated, one of the university museums "placed [the chief's stinger] on display like a piece of rare meat" (ibid, 56). The Meduse, in recognizing the individual and communal trauma of the theft, inflict harm and trauma in the name of their justice. In the following activities, students will have the chance to analyze and critique which knowledge should be pursued and to what extent.

All in all, by embedding Okorafor's *Binti* into the classroom, one could integrate critical analyses of power, privilege, race, and so much more into ELA lessons.

## INSTRUCTIONAL ACTIVITIES

As the genres of science and speculative fiction continuously expand to integrate more than White male protagonists and authors, it has become increasingly vital to reflect deeply on how we—as recipients of these works—treat characters and authors who do not share those racial and gender identities with care thus nurturing a place for folx of color, women, femmes, gender nonconforming folx and others from marginalized communities. The proposed instructional activities offer standard-aligned practices and provide the classroom with an atmosphere of care, play, and concern toward histories and futures that do not normally exist in mainstream classroom.

## BEFORE READING: REIMAGINING AFRICA

### Individual—Journal Prompt: Imagining the Future

This multimodal journal activity activates students' creativity as well as points to future dreaming. Through journaling and discussion, students should leave with an enduring lesson: While science fiction authors produce futures based on their personal knowledge, beliefs, and understandings, there has a predominant notion of who belongs in this future. Nnedi Okorafor, as an Africanfuturist author, reimagines the future where African peoples, cultures, and histories still exist, thrive, and are important to the state of the world see (textbox 10.1).

### TEXTBOX 10.1

### I See (Into) The Future

**Educator Prep:** Collect a series of "futuristic" visuals and scenes. These visuals should encapsulate a wide range of potential environments—urban, rural, underwater, floating island, jungle, desert, technologically advanced or technologically deficient space. These scenes can also be screenshots from popular films such as *Wall-E* (2008), the *Terminator* series (1984–2019), or *The Hunger Games Quartet* (2012–2015).

### Student Directions:

As you scroll and observe the various images, respond to the images in one of the following ways:

- Predict the future based on an image. Answer with a five-sentence story of what could be happening in the scene.
- Contribute to the image by layering the scene with peoples, sounds, and other materials that belong.

### Educator Break-It-Down Prompts:

- What does the world sound like, feel like, look like?
- Who is present in this world? What do the people look like? What behaviors are normalized, permissible, or illegal in this world?
- Who rules or leads this world? What is important as part of this world?

This journaling can be produced through writing, drawing, collaging, recorded oral storytelling, or other modalities that support students in expressing their visions of the future. Once students have produced their work, the teacher can build this output into a whole class activity of a gallery walk (see textbox 10.2).

## TEXTBOX 10.2

### Gallery of Future Past

**Gallery Walk Prep:** Post the following prompts aside various student artifacts to support their critiques and deeper analysis of their peers' work.

**Directions:** Provide students time to silently walk, view, and textually interact with their peers' work via post-it notes or chart paper.

### Prompts:

- Is this vision of the future optimistic, pessimistic, neither or both?
- What assumptions about the future does the author of the work hold?
- Where is this future taking place?

What would you agree with or argue against in this depiction of the vision?

## Small-Group Stations: Africa Past, Present, and Future

This small-group stations' activity is self-directed explorations of narratives regarding Africa's past, present, and future. To support students' performance of this task, divide the classroom in six sections: two sections focused on Africa's past, Africa's present, and Africa in the future.

Educators provide students with the space to analyze various articles, images, and clips that are provided in each station and discuss with their peers. Ideally, students arrive at the enduring understanding: U.S.-centered or West-centered stories often place in the periphery or excise the Global South from the narrative; Okorafor troubles that boundary. Use these stations' conversations as an entry point to discuss the work of Nnedi Okorafor and her objectives as an Africanfuturist writer. Prompt students to explain what these texts may offer as launching pads to rethink and imagine the possibilities of African diaspora in the future.

## Whole-Class Activity—What is Space to a Black Person? To an African?

Consider how little representation there is for Black people in space. This book offers a setting in which Africans can live. Binti's Himba heritage is particularly interesting. Himba are a nomadic people of Namibian origin. The African who makes it into space is from a nomadic people connected to the land (see textbox 10.3).

## TEXTBOX 10.3

### Pop Culture Dive

**Student Directions**: List movies depicting the future. As you are listing, answer these key questions to analyze these films.

**Prompts**:

- What are the key characteristics of those films?
- What predictions of the future hold true across all these texts?
- Who gets to be the protagonist and leads of these stories? Who is usually the antagonist?
- Who gets left out of these stories?

## DURING READING: A HERO'S JOURNEY

### Individual Prompt—Binti Becomes a Hero

Binti begins her hero's journey with the declaration: "No matter what choice [she] made, [she] was never going to have a normal life, really" (Okorafor, 2015, p. 13). In that vein, here are two solo activities students can engage in to deepen their experience with Binti's hero journey.

One activity requires students to analyze Binti's character arc from a self-exiled outcast to a galactic hero. With each new obstacle and experience, prompt students with the following questions in textbox 10.4.

## TEXTBOX 10.4

### Characterization Journal Prompts

**Prompts:**

Is Binti a static or a dynamic character?
How does the moment shift her choices?
Does this moment change her character? If so? How?

An alternative activity is the production of a meme gallery, depicting Binti's hero arc (see textbox 10.5).

## TEXTBOX 10.5

### Traveling Along the Hero's Journey

**Educator Preface:** Using a diagram of a hero's journey, explain the steps that heroes generally take to accomplish a successful arc.

**Prompt:** Explain to students that their gallery should include:

> A meme, the name of the stage the meme represents for Binti, and a caption as to how it captures: a thought, feeling, or action of Binti during a particular phase. Bonus points if the meme and/or caption also alludes to the thoughts, feelings, actions, or dialogues of another party within that stage.

### Small Groups—Elevator Pitch: The Great Negotiator

Amid her journey, Binti discovers her gift as a "master harmonizer," which permits her to negotiate peace to opposing factions. Consequently, students will have a chance to pursue solutions and compromises in the form of elevator pitches.

Prompt: Students produce and present a two-minute speech that shares a solution for any stories' major conflicts to a panel of the novel's characters. A successful speech ultimately produces harmony across all parties, while not conceding either party's nonnegotiables. Each speech should include the following: a recap of the conflict; an analysis of the stakes for each party; a solution; and the intended consequences. This is also a chance for students to question each other's plans.

### Whole-Class Activity—Socratic Seminar: The Hero's Journey

While many Western myths require a hero returns home a changed person, Binti chooses to remain far from home to continue her intellectual pursuits. Furthermore, Binti is transformed as she explains, "I stood there, in my strange body. If I hadn't been deep in meditation I would have screamed and screamed. I was so far from home" (Okorafor, 2015, p. 82). Okorafor's readjustment of the hero's arc requires deeper critical analysis. As such, students should discuss these in a Socratic Seminar.

Socratic Seminar Prompt: Can Binti return home? What are the consequences of her choices in either direction?

Caveat! Whether it was witnessing the murders of friends and strangers or the Meduse-enacted bodily transformation made without her consent, Binti experiences harrowing and traumatic catalysts for change that must be handled with care. As trauma-informed pedagogues, forefront the impending violence and tragedy for students, offer students supports and ways to disengage if needed, and create inquiry spaces to share thoughts, feelings, and questions. Use the prompts below to start critical conversations:

- What were your noticings/observations about the interaction between the Binti and the Meduse chief? What were your feelings about this moment?
- Why would the Meduse's decision to physically change Binti be an issue?
- How would you rewrite this scene to ensure the consent and safety of all participants?
- Do the means justify the end here? The Meduse found and created a mediator in Binti and Binti has made peace and adapted to this fundamental change to her being. Does that justify the lack of consent?

## AFTER READING: HOME/IDENTITY IN AN AFRICANFUTURIST SETTING

As mentioned previously, Binti is consistently grappling with the question of home and belonging throughout her experiences. Consequently, these activities are designed to process how notions of home, belonging, and identity shift and intertwine as one encounters new experiences.

### Individual—What is Home?

Students can free-write answers to the following journal prompts (see textbox 10.6).

---

**TEXTBOX 10.6**

**What is Home?**

**Prompts:**

1. Would you have stayed at the university like Binti, or returned to your family home, or another alternative? Why?
2. How do Binti's cultural background and identity impact her place among the Meduse and within the university? Students may need scaffolds to process the multiple layers of this question. Such scaffolded questions could be: What are some cultural practices that are important to Binti? How do the Meduse respond to Binti's difference? How do the university staff and students respond to her difference?

An alternative activity is a creative project, showcasing *a futuristic society*. Through this project, students will deeply analyze the cultures, histories, and possibilities infused Okorafor's imaginings of an African identity in the future and the place of Africans in the world and galaxy. Second, students will develop various characters' perspectives regarding the importance of space, place, and cultural identity (see textbox 10.7).

---

**TEXTBOX 10.7**

**Tour of Home**

**Prompt:** Throughout *Binti,* various characters cultivate their own visions of home and society. Your project must include a "tour of the universe" from the perspective of primary, secondary, or tertiary character of your choice. The tour may be in the form of a travel brochure, a travel video guide, an elevator pitch, etc. Alongside your creative project is your "curatorial narrative." This artist statement must include quoted evidence from the text that supports the character perspective you have provided as well as reasoning of that text, as well as an explanation of the artistic choices you made to convey your character's perspective. The more detailed the work is, the more engaging the work is.

**Questions for students to consider:**

• What is their character's place in their novel? Are they protagonist, antagonist, antihero, secondary or tertiary character?
• What are their character traits and their motivations?
• What are their views and beliefs about the world that they consider?
• What is their place in the world? Are they pariahs/outcasts? What power do they hold in this society?

---

### Inquiry (Small) Group: Character Web/Character Progression

Over the course of the novel, Binti undergoes a series of life transformations as she decides to leave her native home, witnesses a massacre, becomes a hostage, and then eventually a mediator. To deeply analyze Binti's character, students can produce a body biography. There are myriad ways to create a body biography, but here are suggestions and remixes that would support students in their analysis of home and identities through the work of "Binti" (see textbox 10.8).

---

**TEXTBOX 10.8**

## Mapping out our Characters

**Prompt**: On butcher paper, draw a full-length image of the character you are analyzing. For each body part, answer the appropriate prompt.

- Eyes: What is that person's goal? What is in their line of sight? Who or what do they see?
- Heart: Who or what does the character hold dear and/or love?
- Backbone: What is their motivation? What keeps them standing and moving?
- Hands: What does the character hold in their hands? Literally and figuratively? To be more specific, what tools, experiences, etc. does the character carry with them as part of their way in the world?
- Gut/stomach: What are the character's virtues? What are the character's vices?
- Feet: What are the beliefs they stand on?

Quotations: Pull two to three direct quotes that introduce the character's personality to the audience.

---

A remix of this activity is to have students split the body in half. They will still answer the same questions. However, the left-hand half is a reflection of the character in the beginning before their hero's journey and the right-hand half is a reflection of them at the end of their hero's journey arc. An additional question to further develop the complexity of the Body Biography: ask students to create a home to house the body they drew. Use this question as a prompt: For Binti, based on the first of the novella, what do you think Binti thinks about as her home? With such a temporary ending (as there are two more novellas in this series), there are questions to center a fishbowl discussion with students: Is there a place in this world thus far that Binti can call home? What does that place need to include for Binti to be safe, loved, and included?

## Whole-Class Activity

As mentioned previously, Okorafor is intentional about pursuing a vision of technologically capable and advanced Africa. As such, the possibilities of an Africanfuturistic home are expansive. As a whole class, students can embark on pop culture and media-inquiry session. Due to the growing number of Afro- and Africanfuturistic media, there are suitable choices for all maturity and grade levels.

What do these scenes offer in terms of rethinking what "home" may look like for a future Africa? Media that students can watch include the short film, *Pumzi* (2009) and long-term *Black Panther* (2018). Students can discuss the different images alongside Okorafor-crafted landscape in Binti to think through what Africanfuturism offers as a genre for the notion of identity and home for Africans.

Another whole class option is a fishbowl discussion centering on the experience of the Meduse, regarding the questions of colonization and scientific knowledge. Throughout the text, Okorafor is revealing her perspectives on the present world. What is she telling us through the depiction of this entanglement with the Meduse? How does it mirror past or present moments? As the Meduse are a race of beings who have felt disrespected by the pursuits of others' knowledge, what is their place in this universe? Do they have a home? Do they have a right to protect their home, cultural identities, and traditions at the cost of others' lives and traditions? Does the university have the right to take what they think would help them grow even if it is at the detriment of the other society? Are the actions of the colonized/oppressed justified? Maybe we can talk about this while keeping in mind how this impacts current realities?

## CONCLUSION

I end with a brief snapshot of in-process reflections. As a Nigerian-American woman, Nnedi Okorafor's characters, storylines, and world-building supported me in navigating and owning my transnational Blackness. As such, the activities here are informed by and written from such experiences, knowledge, and perspectives, as well as from my own pedagogies as an educator.

If, as educators, we do not do a deep and vulnerable self-reflection before introducing these texts, the activities will not lift off as they could. At best, they will remain flat or empty and at worst, they will harm. If you embrace Binti and her compatriots in your classroom, I hope it is with the utmost care and diligence to people and stories that are so often placed in the periphery.

## REFERENCES

D'arcy, P. (2018, October 17). "Write your story, and don't be afraid to write it"—A sci-fi writer talks about finding her voice and being a superhero. *Ideas.Ted. Com*. https://ideas.ted.com/write-your-story-and-dont-be-afraid-to-write-it-a-sci-fi-writer-talks-about-finding-her-voice-and-being-a-superhero/

Duffy, D., Jennings, J., & Butler, O. (2017). *Kindred: A graphic novel adaptation.* Abrams Comicarts.

*Locus Magazine.* (2021, May 10). Nnedi Okorafor: That which is hers. *Locus Online.* https://locusmag.com/2021/05/nnedi-okorafor-that-which-is-hers/

Okorafor, N. (2010). *Who fears death.* DAW Books Inc.

Okorafor, N. (2015). *Binti.* Tom Doherty Associates.

Okorafor, N. (2017, August). Transcript of "Sci-fi stories that imagine a future Africa." https://www.ted.com/talks/nnedi_okorafor_sci_fi_stories_that_imagine _a_future_africa/transcript

Okorafor, N. (2019, October 19). Africanfuturism defined. http://nnedi.blogspot.com /2019/10/africanfuturism-defined.html

*Chapter 11*

# Lamar Giles

## *Exploring the Ins and Outs of Community in* Not So Pure and Simple

### Morgan Jackson

Lamar Giles writes the kind of novels he wanted to read as a teen and young adult (YA). He is a two-time Edgar Award finalist for his first two YA novels, *Fake ID* and *Endangered*, and has received acclaim for both his YA and middle-grade novels. His work consistently receives glowing reviews and appears on "Best Of" lists. On top of his production of novels, Giles also frequently contributes to anthologies.

Giles is not just an author; he is an activist too. His novels tell enthralling stories that capture the mind and attention of the reader, but are also unapologetically about Black kids. In his own words, he says "while anybody can enjoy [his books], they are not about generic avatars; [they] are about Black kids." Giles is also a founding member of We Need Diverse Books which further indicates his commitment to the representation of Black kids in YA and middle-grade literature.

An emphasis of We Need Diverse Books and Giles's work is to show a nuanced view of what it means to be a Black teen in America. He does so in a way that shies away from the expected, identity-trauma stories to display authentic and relatable representations. This is particularly present in the focus text for this chapter, *Not So Pure and Simple*. In telling the story of Del, Kiera, and other current and former students of Green Creek High, he provides insight into the complicated world of adolescence.

## CRITICAL DISCUSSION OF *NOT SO PURE AND SIMPLE*

Although Giles has written other YA novels, *Not So Pure and Simple* is his
first contemporary YA title. It is firmly a YA novel perhaps best suited for
high schoolers, but quite possibly enjoyed by middle schoolers in an environment that welcomes difficult questions and willingly engages in and provokes
honest conversations. *Not So Pure and Simple* received five starred reviews
from publications and was heralded for its authentic portrayal of teenage
life. Most of the novel focuses on sexuality and sexual identity as portrayed
in Del's struggle for a balance between his purity classes at church and his
healthy living class at school.

The conflicts in the story center on sexual education, but in many ways it is
less about sexuality and more about who should be making educational decisions for students. The church, First Missionary House of the Lord, is heavily involved in what should be taught, who should be teaching it, and what
students should be allowed to take the course. While this story is about sex
education, it could just as easily be about any topic that an organized religion
or specific religious institution may take issues with.

Giles's realistic portrayal of adolescent sexuality is front and center highlighting how sexuality is complicated by familial relationships, parent expectations, religion, and society. Giles is not gratuitous in his depiction of the
sexual education activity. He treats it with the caution it deserves and depicts
the myriad of issues adolescents face when dealing with sexuality including
the expectations and stigmas parents attach, sometimes even unknowingly.
Adolescents will recognize the issues and dilemmas the characters face while
adults can gain insight into these cumbersome experiences and help the
young people in their lives navigate them.

## INSTRUCTIONAL ACTIVITIES FOR
## *NOT SO PURE AND SIMPLE*

Sex education, sexual identity, and sexual activities are the crux of *Not
So Pure and Simple*. Any conversation surrounding this novel will have
to address those topics and a myriad of tangential topics as well. Teachers
are cautioned to be cognizant of their own school communities and school
expectations when engaging in classroom discussions and activities. Despite
a seemingly overwhelming sexual content, there are a number of other topics
to be discussed in regards to *Not So Pure and Simple* and it would be a dis-
service to the novel and Giles himself to ignore those topics.

What proceeds from here are a variety of ELA activities to be completed
throughout the reading process (before, during, and after) as well as activities

that can be completed as a whole class, in small groups, or as individual assignments. Similarly, some of the activities are intended to be completed in a finite period of time whereas others can be continued throughout the reading or for an extended period of time. The activities included are meant to be used as starting points. They can and should be adjusted to the needs of the students and teachers. Some activities can be used to build into others, but can also be used individually.

## BEFORE READING

### Individual

In many ways, this story looks at the various ways in which people are included and excluded from a community. It also looks at the intersectionality of communities and identities. Readers embark on a journey with the characters and will likely find themselves learning and questioning right alongside Del, Kiera, Jameer, and Qwan.

Teachers can facilitate this growth by having students identify all the communities they belong to. Students may struggle in the beginning to come up with those beyond the obvious "student," "child," "sibling," "friend," but ask them to think about things that are formally organized and they participate in (memberships, organizations, clubs, teams, etc.). Then educators should draw their attention to the communities the students may belong to that do not require an active participation, that is, adopted, cancer survivor, racial or religious identities, and so on.

The things listed above are meant to serve as examples, but are absolutely not all-inclusive. Once the lists have been made, ask students to identify how membership in the said community is defined or how one becomes a member of the group. Teachers can facilitate a conversation about what it means to be a member of a particular group and if all members are equal.

There is no right or wrong to this activity. It is meant to allow students to think critically and imaginatively about how membership is navigated. Conversation will be more robust if students have already considered the contraindications of their membership, meaning does belonging to one group conflict with being a member of another group? The whole-group activity below can be used in conjunction with this one, either before or after students complete the individual activity.

### Small Group

The main point of contention in the novel is the enmeshment between the church's First Missionary House of the Lord and its pastor, Pastor Newsome, with the school board and curriculum decisions at Green Creek High. The pastor's involvement on the curriculum committee led to the church being able to counter the school's *Healthy Living* course with their own purity course and ultimately led to the school's course being canceled mid-semester.

The most direct correlation is for students to investigate their own local school boards and research things like (1) who makes curriculum decisions, (2) how those people are chosen, (3) who is responsible for the district's sex-ed program, and or (4) who selects or approves textbooks? Groups could research all four or these four topics could be split among the groups.

If an educator is uncomfortable or unable to have students investigate their local school board/district policies, this activity can be amended to focus instead on the concept of "separation between church and state" as outlined in the First Amendment of the U.S. Constitution. Before reading the novel, students can consider the influence religion has or should have on community decisions; this does not have to be related solely to education and educational practices.

After a brief introduction by the teacher, small groups of students should work together to explain what Jefferson actually says in the Constitution in regards to Church and State. Teachers can then provide students with a topic to be researched within the group and determine whether or not it qualifies as a violation of the separation between the two institutes. Possible topics to be researched include (1) the use of the Bible to swear on in a court of law, (2) the inclusion of "one nation, under God" in the "Pledge of Allegiance," (3) "In God We Trust" being printed on U.S. money, and 4) the removal of prayer from schools in 1962.

Regardless of which way students complete this activity, their results can be shared with the class and referred back to as Pastor Newsome's full involvement in the school curriculum unfolds in the story.

## Whole Class

Though it is not named until nearly the end of the novel, the idea of community is really quite central to the story Giles tells. *Not So Pure and Simple* does not offer a definition of community or rules for being a member of a community. In fact, Giles constantly sets up situations in which the characters are asking themselves those very questions.

As a whole class, students should investigate their school. First, the class will need to make a list of everyone who is or can be considered a member of the school community, by role/title, not name. This should be an exhaustive list of anyone and everyone who is a member of the community. While teachers, students, and administrators are likely to be easy to come up with, educators should push their students to think beyond those and include people like lunch workers, maintenance, custodians, bus drivers, landscapers, coaches, secretaries and receptionists, and parents.

Once the list has been made students should identify (1) how each person contributes to the community, (2) rank each member in terms of importance, and (3) rank each member in terms of value or power. The ranking can be done whole group or individually and then shared out with the class. Students should be reminded to be respectful and that these rankings are a matter of perspective and personal opinion. How students rank these positions might be different if members of the others groups were doing the ranking.

With these things done a conversation can be had about how students determined the value and importance of each member. If it has not already come up earlier, ask students if all members in each group are equal. Do all students rank the same for importance and power? If so, why is that? If not, what determines more or less importance or power? These same questions can be asked for each group identified.

The idea is for students to begin thinking about social hierarchies and the intersectionality of identities as they begin reading. The ideas that come up in conversation should be jotted down so they can be referred to throughout the reading allowing students to track how their thoughts align with their views as they read.

## DURING READING

### Individual

Although Del is the main character of the story, many of the supporting characters are round and dynamic, meaning they are depicted as complete characters with growth and insight into the characters' motivations. For this activity, the teacher can assign students a character to follow throughout the reading or allow students to select a character from the list provided (see textbox 11.1).

### TEXTBOX 11.1 CHARACTER LIST

Del
Kiera
Jameer
Pastor Newsome
Cressie
Qwan
MJ
Shianne

As the class reads, students will create six-word stories for their assigned or chosen character throughout the reading. A six-word story is a compilation of six words, not necessarily a sentence, but more than just a list of six words, that convey a complete opinion or thought about the topic, in this case a character.

Direct students that the goal of their six-word story is to convey meaning, explain character motives, or provide character analysis. Students should not use the character's name in their six-word story. It should be apparent who the character is, but not stated. For example, a six-word story about *Cinderella* could look something like this: "Chores, chores, chores; nothing else matters" which focuses on Cinderella's constant role as the cleaner of her household. A six-word story like "Doormat: used, because she allows it" would also work as it indicates a reader's perspective that Cinderella's real issue is she allows herself to be mistreated, not the actual mistreatment.

Providing helpful tips and guidelines with students in advance of creating their six-word stories can make the task more manageable (see textbox 11.2). Students may require some practice prior to being ready to do this activity. As a warm-up, students can create six-word stories about themselves, their school, or a common knowledge story. This can be done individually, with partners, in small groups, or with the class as a whole.

## TEXTBOX 11.2

### Six-Word Stories

| Rules for Six-Word Stories | Tips for Six-Word Stories |
|---|---|
| • Must be six words (symbols count as words if you say them).<br>• Cannot include the subject.<br>• Must be an opinion.<br>• Is not a sentence.<br>• Cannot be a list of six words. | • Focus on what is important about the topic.<br>• Stick to one point about the topic.<br>• Write what comes to mind and then edit for the rules.<br>• Don't erase, just cross out.<br>• Try to convey more than what the six words say. |

For this activity it is easier to divide the reading into sections; the goal being for students to create such a story that depicts the character during the assigned sections. A possible breakdown can be found in textbox 11.3. The teacher can assign a six-word story more or less frequently, as they see fit. As the story progresses, students can also focus their six-word story on the changes of the character. Educators should note that this activity is intended to have students thinking critically about the characters through an analysis of the character's words, actions, and interactions with other characters.

**TEXTBOX 11.3 SUGGESTED CHAPTER BREAKDOWN FOR ASSIGNMENTS**

| Section | Chapters |
|---------|----------|
| 1. | 1–4 |
| 2. | 5–12 |
| 3. | 13–18 |
| 4. | 19–22 |
| 5. | 23–28 |
| 6. | 29–31 |

One way to grow students as they work on six-word stories over the course of a longer work, such as this novel, is to have students share their stories with each other and try to guess which character the story is about. Teachers can also put one on the board and have the class try to guess the character. Additionally, students can be tasked with finding quotes from the story to support their, or a classmate's, six-word story thus reinforcing the writing skills they have likely worked on in class.

## Small Group

For the small-group activity, teachers can use the same chapter breakdown from the individual activity (see textbox 11.3). This allows the teacher to create mini-units from the novel and will only require the teacher to remember one reading schedule for activities.

As the story unfolds many of the characters deal with personal struggles and issues. Despite having friends and family, they often handle their issues on their own. For this assignment, students will write to an advice columnist (e.g., Dear Abby or Dear Prudence) for help with an issue they are currently facing.

If the class is also doing the individual activity above, students can be grouped by the character they were assigned for it. If that activity is not being completed see textbox 11.1 for a list of characters students can choose from or be assigned. Teachers can adjust group sizes to their own classroom needs. They may also keep students in the same groups for each assigned section or create new groups, assigning new characters for each reading. Similarly, educators can determine if they want to provide students with the characters at the beginning of a new section or at the end of the section.

For this activity, students should create a letter seeking help for an issue. Students will tailor their letters to what is currently happening in the story. They can add any additional information to the letter based on their understanding of the character. Students' letters should begin with background information. This information should come from the story, but can also be infused with information the student has come to understand or surmise from their reading.

The letter should end with a specific question the character is asking for help with and be signed with an eponym, or a name that is indicative of the problem the character has just divulged. Textbox 11.4 provides a sample letter that may help students to understand the activity. This sample letter can be shared with students or used as a mini-lesson prior to completing this activity.

If looking for an extension activity, teachers can swap letters among groups and have the students write replies with answers to the questions asked. The sample provided in textbox 11.4 includes a response which may help students formulate their own responses. If utilizing this extension, teachers can make multiple copies thus allowing students to respond individually and then rate or vote on the best response to the letter.

## TEXTBOX 11.4

### Sample Advice and Response Letter

| *Sample Letter* | *Sample Response* |
| --- | --- |
| Dear Ms. Jackson,<br>I am quite lonely. My father died, leaving me with my stepmother and stepsisters. I don't mind that part so much, but they don't like me. I thought we could be friends but they just ask me to do all their chores. I don't mind helping them. I just thought that if I did enough to help them they would start inviting me to hang out with them. That hasn't been the case. How do I get them to see me more as a friend and less as a maid? | Dear Tired,<br>Friends like you for who you are not for what you can do for them. This applies to family as well. If your stepsisters are unwilling to be your friend you should stop doing things for them. Your current behavior will only give them permission to continue to mistreat you. Whether or not they are willing to see it, you must see your own worth. You cannot change how others treat you, but you can determine how you treat yourself. |
| Tired of Cooking and Cleaning for my Evil Stepsisters (Cinderella, though students should not include their character's name) | Ms. Jackson |

## Whole Group

As discussed earlier, there is a great sense of community or lack thereof in the story. So much of the plot of *Not So Pure and Simple* centers around who is considered *inside* and who is considered *outside* the various communities. Two of the before-reading activities asked students to consider their community memberships and what they mean separately and as a part of the whole. This same activity can be done with the characters from the novel.

Teachers will need to dedicate a space to keep track of the communities depicted in the text and the characters' interaction, acceptance, and rejection within those communities. This space can be chart paper on the wall or board or an electronic document that can be shared with students, but also edited, revised, and updated over time. It is important to ensure that students have access to this document as it will come in handy for the individual activity outlined below.

Using the reading schedule provided in textbox 11.3, class discussions should be held at the end of each section. As they read, students should be asked to keep track of the communities that are depicted during that section (e.g., Green Creek High School, First Missionary House of the Lord, Monte FISHto'S, Baby-Getters Club, Purity Pledge, Healthy Living class). This list is not exhaustive, but provides a good idea of just how broad or specific the communities can be.

During class discussions, students are encouraged to share the communities they noticed. If a teacher notices that students are struggling to identify the communities they can elect to share them with students or assign groups to review certain chapters looking for communities.

Each community identified should be depicted with a circle (large enough to write inside). The title of the community can go above or below the circle. Inside of the circle, students should list the characters who are members of that community. On the edge of the circle, so that it appears both within and outside of the circle, write the characters who are straddling the boundaries of membership. Lastly, outside of the circle should be characters who are not members of the community.

At the conclusion of each section, check to see if more communities need to be added. Then, discuss the placement of the character, that is, within, on the edge, or outside of the circle. For each class discussion and section of reading, use a different color ink, or font, so that it is easier to see the characters' movements of membership. It is possible that students will disagree with where some of the characters belong, which is fine. This should be resolved by referring back to the story for textual support of character placement. They can determine if there needs to be a definitive placement or if it is possible to place a character in more than one location.

## AFTER READING

### Individual

This activity most naturally follows the whole class, during the reading activity. It is, however, entirely possible for students to complete this activity without doing that one. After reading the story students should be prepared to discuss the various ways in which community impacts individuals both in real life and in the text.

Assign students a written activity in which they determine the message Giles conveys about community, such as "Throughout the novel the concept of community is discussed including what it takes to be accepted and/or rejected as a member of those communities. What do you believe is the text's message about community? You are welcome to interpret 'community' in any manner that you believe aligns with the novel. You are not talking about a specific community, but the idea of community as a whole. Use evidence from the text to support your thesis." This prompt can be modified to align with classroom discussions.

There is no right or wrong answer here, it is more so for students to reflect on what they have learned about the community, its intersections, and rules for membership or exclusion. This can be done as a timed write in class or a more formal essay, depending on the needs and limitations of the classroom.

### Small Group

At the beginning of the novel, Del and Qwan spend a lot of time discussing their sexual escapades. As the novel wraps up, Cressie confesses her harrowing experience in college as well as what other viewers/listeners shared with her. There is even an outright conversation about the teenage girls who have gotten pregnant and the double standard of how they are treated/shunned in contrast to the fathers of their children who have remained mostly anonymous and unscathed despite engaging in the same behavior, with the same outcome.

All of these events are ripe for class discussion and conversation. Instead of focusing on the hot-button topics of sexuality, sexual identity, and orientation, students can investigate the often contradictory and hypocritical depictions of femininity and masculinity both within the book and in real life. Students can be assigned a list of topics (see textbox 11.5) the teacher can create their own list, or students can be given the opportunity to determine their own research topic.

## TEXTBOX 11.5

### Possible Topics for Research

Discriminatory pricing on products and services for women (pink tax)
Pay disparity between men and women
Clothing disparity for boys and girls
Rape culture on college campuses
Slut shaming, differences in how genders' sexual activity is viewed
Gender stereotyping of emotions

The goal of the project is to look into the reality of the gender double standard that runs throughout the novel. Each group should create a presentation on their topic and how it relates to or connects with *Not So Pure and Simple*. A rubric for the project/presentation can be found in textbox 11.6.

## TEXTBOX 11.6

### Sample Project Rubric

| | 10 | 8 | 6 |
|---|---|---|---|
| **Research** | The topic is thoroughly explained. Research conducted explains the various aspects of the issue at hand, and provides a clear depiction of the issues from all sides. | The topic has been researched. Some information is provided and offers insight into the issue, but lacks details or a complete overview of the topic. | Minimum research has been done. Little more than a summary is provided. |
| **Presentation** | Careful attention is paid to the aesthetics of the presentation. Font size, style, and color as well as images enhance the presentation. | The presentation is well put together and has a good aesthetic appearance; however, the font choices and/or images do not enhance the presentation. | The presentation provides little in the way of aesthetics. It lacks images or creative font choices. |
| **Connection to novel** | Clear and explicit connections are made between the information researched and the novel. Information from the novel is clearly and accurately cited. | The researched information is mostly connected to the novel, but sometimes requires the audience to make their own inferences. | The focus is on the information researched with little connection to the novel. What connections are made are lacking, incorrect, or missing citations. |

## Whole Group

Once the book is finished students will likely have opinions about the issues, the characters, and the outcomes of the various storylines. A fitting whole-group activity once the novel has concluded is a carefully crafted class discussion.

Give each student a notecard or post-it note and direct them to write a question that stems from the novel on it. In a technologically advanced classroom, students can complete a Google form with their questions or add them to a shared Google Doc. Students should be guided that the question is not intended to be about the plot of the story, but the concepts and ideas. They can also come up with questions connecting the concepts from the novel to the real world.

Arrange students in a circle or square, which will allow for all students to be visible to each other. As the teacher, prepare some questions that can be used to get the students talking and maintain a good conversation. To start the conversation, teachers can ask students "Cressie's confession about her experience with the guy at the party brings up the idea of toxic masculinity. Del immediately disagrees that he is nothing like that guy and that his behavior was not toxic. What do you think about Del's behavior toward Kiera? In what ways was it toxic? In what ways wasn't it?" For additional questions check out textbox 11.7 at the end of this chapter.

---

### TEXTBOX 11.7

### Classroom Discussion questions

- Cressie's confession about her experience with the guy at the party brings up the idea of toxic masculinity. Del immediately disagrees that he is nothing like that guy and that his behavior was not toxic. What do you think about Del's behavior toward Kiera? In what ways was it toxic? In what ways wasn't it?
- The parents of the Purity Pledges do not allow them to participate in the healthy living class at school. They resort to asking Del to get answers to their "personal" questions. Should parents be allowed to determine what classes their high school students can take? Why or why not?
- Jameer's parents are very strict about his use of technology. They refuse to give him a phone that can go online. His computer is in the middle of the living room, and his bedroom has no door. Would you consider his parents abusive? Why or why not?
- Del and Shianne have a complicated history. What is your opinion about the secret they've kept for all this time?
- What are your thoughts on *The Baby-getters Club*? Why would people believe this story versus the truth?
- What do you think of the way the parents in the story were depicted? Is it accurate or inaccurate? Why?
- What are your thoughts about the First Missionary House of the Lord?

If the teacher would like to hold students accountable during the discussion they can either track student comments to ensure participation or ask students to complete a quick timed write on one of the topics or questions from the discussion.

## CONCLUSION

*Not So Pure and Simple* provides adolescents a story they connect to in a myriad of ways. Educators looking to use it in the classroom may be concerned given its focus on sexuality and sex education; however, Giles's story creates a variety of avenues for teachers and students to engage. The activities included here are intended to be used to move students beyond the obvious topics and to get them to think deeper and investigate character's motives as well as connect elements of the novel to the real world. Many of these activities can be modified to fit the parameters and expectations of various classroom settings.

# About the Editors

## STEVE T. BICKMORE

**Steven T. Bickmore** is a professor of English Education at UNLV and maintains a weekly academic blog on young adult (YA) literature (http://www
.yawednesday.com/). He is a past editor of *The ALAN Review* (2009–2014) and a founding editor of *Study and Scrutiny: Research in Young Adult Literature*. He maintains a weekly academic blog on YA Literature—Dr. Bickmore's YA Wednesday (http://www.yawednesday.com/). This academic blog offers a space for academics, teachers, librarians, and students to discuss scholarship and trends in YA literature. His research interests include the induction and mentoring of novice teachers and how preservice and novice English teachers negotiate the teaching of literature using YA literature, especially around the issues of race, class, and gender. His publications have appeared in such journals as *English Education*, *The English Journal*, *The ALAN Review*, *The SIGNAL Journal*, and *Taboo*.

## SHANETIA P. CLARK

**Shanetia P. Clark, PhD**, is an associate professor of literacy in the Department of Early and Elementary Education at Salisbury University in Salisbury, Maryland. She holds a bachelor's degree in English and a masters in teaching degree from the University of Virginia. She attended graduate school at the Pennsylvania State University, where she earned a PhD in curriculum and instruction, with an emphasis in language and literacy education. Her interests include young adult and children's literature, the exploration of aesthetic experiences within reading and writing classrooms, and writing pedagogy. She has published peer-reviewed articles and books chapters within these professional interests. She has published in journals such as *The Journal of Language and Literacy*, *International Journal of Learning*, *The ALAN Review*, and *The SIGNAL Journal*. She teaches courses in children's literature, creative arts in literacy, and language arts methods. In addition, Dr. Clark supervises interns in local schools.

# About the Authors

## OLUWASEUN ANIMASHAUN

**Oluwaseun Animashaun** is a doctoral student in the Department of Curriculum and Teaching at Teachers College, Columbia University, as well as a sixth grade English Language Arts Teacher in New York. Her current research interests are pop culture, play, and speculative futures. When she is not in the classroom, you can find her binging the newest Netflix drop or speed-reading through the latest young adult novel.

## WANDA M. BROOKS

**Wanda M. Brooks** is an associate professor in the Department of Teaching and Learning at Temple University. She coordinates all of the middle grades teacher certification programs in the College. She teaches courses related to literacy theories, research and instruction, as well as qualitative research methods.

## DAWAN COOMBS

**Dawan Coombs** is an associate professor of English at Brigham Young University. Her teaching and research interests focus on reader identity and pedagogy as well as young adult literature. She has served as a member of the International Reading Association Children's and Young Adults' Book Award Committee.

## ALEX CORBITT

**Alex Corbitt** (@Alex_Corbitt) is a doctoral student at Boston College's Lynch School of Education and Human Development. His research interests include literacies, game-based learning, and speculative fiction. Before enrolling at Boston College, Alex taught literacy at a public middle school in the Bronx, New York. You can learn more about Alex's work at alexcorbitt.com.

## BRYAN RIPLEY CRANDALL

**Bryan Ripley Crandall** is the director of the Connecticut Writing Project and an associate professor of English education at Fairfield University. His dissertation, *"A Responsibility to Speak Out": Perspectives on Writing From Black African-Born Males With Limited and Disrupted Formal Education*, received a Syracuse University doctoral prize for outstanding research. Crandall's scholarship has appeared in several journals and books, advocating for best practices for teaching writing in diverse, inclusive settings. In 2018, Crandall received a Divergent Award from the Initiative for Literacy in a Digital Age in recognition of his youth programming, including Ubuntu Academy—a literacy lab for immigrant and refugee youth.

## DESIREE CUETO

**Desiree Cueto** is an assistant professor in the Department of Elementary Education at Western Washington University. She is the director of the Pacific Northwest Children's Literature Clearinghouse and teaches courses in children's literature and language arts methods. She also serves as a chair of the NCTE Charlotte Huck Award for Outstanding Fiction for Children and is a section editor for the *AERA Handbook of Research on Teachers of Color*.

## SHIMIKQUA E. ELLIS

**Shimikqua E. Ellis**, PhD, is an assistant professor for the English education DA program at Murray State University. Dr. Ellis has also trained educators for Teach for America and The University of Mississippi. Her interests include multicultural young adult literature, culturally responsive pedagogies, and social justice education.

## MORGAN JACKSON

**Morgan Jackson** is a high school English teacher in Las Vegas, Nevada. She is a member of NCTE and ALAN. Her current ALAN commitments include serving on the Amelia E. Walden book award committee and chair of the Equity, Diversity, and Inclusion Committee. She is committed to students growing through their reading and providing equitable representation for all students.

## KIMBERLY N. PARKER

**Dr. Kimberly N. Parker** is currently the director of the Crimson Summer Academy at Harvard University. Kim, who was a successful classroom teacher for 20 years, is the 2020 recipient of the National Council of Teachers of English (NCTE) Outstanding Elementary Educator Award; a cofounder of #DisruptTexts and #31DaysIBPOC; and the current president of the Black Educators' Alliance of MA (BEAM). Her book with the Association for Curriculum and Supervision Development (ASCD), *Literacy is Liberation: Working Toward Justice Through Culturally Relevant Teaching*, is published in February 2022. Follow her on Twitter at @TchKimpossible.

## DANI RIMBACH-JONES

**Dani Rimbach-Jones** was a former high school English teacher for Clark County School District in Las Vegas, Nevada. She was a graduate of an International Baccalaureate program as a high school student and then spent much of her teaching career teaching English within the International Baccalaureate program supporting a wide variety of students. She is currently a doctoral student at the University of Tennessee, Knoxville, focusing her studies on young adult literature in English classrooms.

## GRETCHEN RUMOHR

**Gretchen Rumohr** (ghr001@aquinas.edu) is a professor of English and department chair at Aquinas College, where she teaches writing and language arts methods. She is also the current chief curator of Dr. Bickmore's YA Wednesday blog (http://www.yawednesday.com/) and is a codirector of the UNLV Summit on the research and teaching of young adult literature. She lives with her four girls and a five-pound Yorkshire Terrier in west Michigan.

Lightning Source UK Ltd.
Milton Keynes UK
UKHW012340130622
404369UK00002B/46